THE ROVER BOYS IN ALASKA

OR

LOST IN THE FIELDS OF ICE

BY

ARTHUR M. WINFIELD

AUTHOR OF "THE ROVER BOYS AT SCHOOL," "THE ROVER BOYS ON THE OCEAN," "THE PUTNAM HALL SERIES," ETC.

ILLUSTRATED

NEW YORK
GROSSET & DUNLAP
PUBLISHERS

BOOKS BY ARTHUR M. WINFIELD

THE ROVER BOYS SERIES

THE ROVER BOYS AT SCHOOL
THE ROVER BOYS ON THE OCEAN
THE ROVER BOYS IN THE JUNGLE
THE ROVER BOYS OUT WEST
THE ROVER BOYS ON THE GREAT LAKES
THE ROVER BOYS IN THE MOUNTAINS
THE ROVER BOYS IN CAMP
THE ROVER BOYS ON LAND AND SEA
THE ROVER BOYS ON THE RIVER
THE ROVER BOYS ON THE PLAINS
THE ROVER BOYS IN SOUTHERN WATERS
THE ROVER BOYS ON THE FARM
THE ROVER BOYS ON TREASURE ISLE
THE ROVER BOYS AT COLLEGE
THE ROVER BOYS DOWN EAST
THE ROVER BOYS IN THE AIR
THE ROVER BOYS IN NEW YORK
THE ROVER BOYS IN ALASKA

(Other volumes in preparation)

THE PUTNAM HALL SERIES

THE PUTNAM HALL CADETS
THE PUTNAM HALL RIVALS
THE PUTNAM HALL CHAMPIONS
THE PUTNAM HALL REBELLION
THE PUTNAM HALL ENCAMPMENT
THE PUTNAM HALL MYSTERY

12mo. Cloth. Illustrated.
Price, per volume, 60 cents, postpaid.

GROSSET & DUNLAP, Publishers, New York

The Rover Boys in Alaska

INTRODUCTION

My Dear Boys: This book is a complete story in itself, but forms the eighteenth volume in a line issued under the general title of "The Rover Boys Series for Young Americans."

As I have mentioned in some of the other volumes, this line was started with the publication of "The Rover Boys at School," "On the Ocean," and "In the Jungle." The books were so well received that they were followed, year after year, by the publication of "The Rover Boys Out West," "On the Great Lakes," "In Camp," "On Land and Sea," "On the River," "On the Plains," "In Southern Waters," "On the Farm," "On Treasure Isle," "At College," "Down East," "In the Air," and then "In New York," where we last met the lads.

The boys are growing older—as all boys do—and Dick is married, and helping his father in business. In the present story Sam and Tom return to college, until something quite out of the ordinary occurs and the fun-loving Tom disappears most mysteriously. Sam and Dick go in search of their brother, and the trail leads them to far-away Alaska, where they encounter many perils in the fields of ice and snow.

The publishers assure me that by the end of the present year the total of sales on this series of books will have reached *one million and a half copies!* This is, to me, truly amazing, and I cannot help but feel profoundly grateful to all the boys and girls, and their parents, who have taken such an interest in my stories. I trust with all my heart that the reading of the books will do the young folks good.

Affectionately and sincerely yours,

ARTHUR M. WINFIELD.

CONTENTS

THE ROVER BOYS IN ALASKA

CHAPTER I

TOM AND SAM

"WELL, here we are again, Tom, down to the grind of college life."

"That's right, Sam. Not so much fun as attending a wedding, is it?" And Tom Rover grinned broadly at his brother.

"We can't expect to go to weddings all the time," returned Sam Rover, a grin showing on his own face. "Wonder how Dick and Dora are making out," he mused.

"Oh, fine, you can be sure of that. Dora is just the girl for Dick."

"How do you like being back here, Tom?" and the youngest Rover looked anxiously at his brother.

Tom heaved a deep sigh before replying.

"To tell the truth, Sam, I wish I had stayed home a bit longer," he said slowly. "My head isn't just as clear as it might be. That whack

Pelter gave me with that footstool was an awful one."

"It certainly was, and it's a wonder it didn't split your skull open. Maybe you'd better go back home for a rest."

"Oh, no, it isn't as bad as that. Sometimes I feel a bit dizzy, that's all. But I guess that will wear away, sooner or later. You see, I've been studying hard the last three days, trying to make up for lost time, and that is what's done it. I think I'll take it a bit easier after this, until I feel more like myself."

"Don't you think you had better see a doctor?"

"No, I've had the doctor fussing over me until I am tired of it. What I need is some fun, Sam. Can't you think of something? Whenever I try to concoct some sort of a joke it makes my head ache," and poor Tom, who loved to play pranks as much as ever, heaved another sigh.

"Let us take a long walk this afternoon, Tom. Maybe that will do your head some good. We can take Songbird and some of the others along."

"All right; anything to get out of the greasy grind of studying. My! don't I wish I was in Dick's place and didn't have to go to college any more!"

"Well, Dick's got his hands full with Dad's business. Those brokers left things in a perfect mess."

"I know it. But Dick will straighten things out—he's got a head for just that sort of thing." Tom took up a text book, glanced at it for a moment, and then threw it on the table. "No use, I can't study any more to-day. I'm going out on the campus. You come a soon as you are done and we'll take that walk."

"All right. Will you tell Songbird and whoever else you want to go along?"

"Yes," answered Tom, and without further words he took up his cap, heaved another deep sigh, and left the room. Sam watched his brother pass down the corridor of the college building and noted that he placed his hand to the back of his head and kept it there for some time.

"Poor Tom!" murmured the youngest Rover, as he turned again to the lesson he had been studying. "He tries to keep up a brave front, but that crack he got on the head some weeks ago was a worse one than most folks imagine. I'm thinking he ought to be home and under the doctor's care instead of trying to rack his brains making up lessons he missed while we were away."

Tom passed along the corridor until he had

turned a corner and was out of sight of the room he and Sam occupied. Then he looked around to make certain that nobody was observing him. Both of his hands went up to the back of his head and he clenched his teeth hard.

"What *is* the matter with this old head of mine!" he murmured. "Sometimes I feel as if I had a regular windmill inside of it. And when I try to study it gets to be a regular blank. Something is wrong, that's certain. What is it?"

He stood in the corner of the corridor for several minutes, trying to pull himself together, mentally and physically. His face was still somewhat pale, from the suffering he had undergone, since the time a wooden footstool hurled by an enemy had hit him and knocked him unconscious.

"Rats! this won't do!" he finally exclaimed, and shaking himself, he hurried out of the building and on to the broad, velvety college campus.

Students were walking in various directions, going to, or coming from, classes and lectures. Many hailed him and he called out in return, or waved his hand. The Rover boys had a host of friends at Brill.

Presently Tom saw a tall, slim young man coming up, dressed in a light, checked suit, and wearing pointed patent-leather ties and a rose-colored cap. In the buttonhole of the student was a large carnation. Under his arm the approaching one carried half a dozen text books.

The face of the fun-loving Rover lighted up and for the time being the pain in his head was forgotten. His hand went down in a pocket, to feel for something, and then came forth again. Then he stepped forward and crooked out his elbow.

The other student was looking to one side as he came forward and he did not notice the elbow in his way. The elbow caught him in the ribs, causing him to give a grunt, and the armful of books were scattered on the walk.

"My gracious me!" gasped the stylishly-dressed youth. "What did you do that for, Tom Rover?"

"Sorry, Tubblets," answered Tom, making as sober a face as possible. "I didn't know you wanted the whole walk."

"You did that on purpose, Tom Rover, you know you did!"

"Did what on purpose, Tubby?"

"How many times must I tell you that my name is not Tubby or Tubblets. It is William Philander Tubbs, and I want you to call me by my right name after this."

"Very well, Mr. W. P. Washbasin—I mean Tubbs. I'll not forget again," and Tom made a low bow.

"And I don't want you to knock my books out of my arm again," went on William Philander, drawing himself up disdainfully.

"Your books, Willie?"

"Yes, my books," came wrathfully from the dudish student. "And don't you dare to call me Willie. My name is——"

"Oh, yes, I remember now, Philugger."

"It's not Philugger, either. It is Wil——"

"Sure, I know, Philliam Tubbander Williams. Sorry I forgot before." And Tom looked truly sorrowful.

"Oh, you are simply horrid, that's what you are!" declared the stylishly-dressed student, in despair. "And my books are all covered with dirt!"

"I beg a million pardons," cried Tom, and started to pick the books up, one after another. As he did this one hand went again into that pocket before mentioned and, on the sly, he inserted a printed sheet of paper into each book. "Now you are all fixed, Tubbly," he added. "And you can run along to school like a nice little boy. But wait a moment till I fix your collar," he went on, as he turned the other youth around.

"What's the matter with my collar?" demanded the dudish student, suspiciously.

"Talcum powder, I guess. You mustn't use so much after this." And Tom commenced to brush the collar vigorously.

"I—er—I didn't use much—just a little for my nose, don't you know," answered William Philander Tubbs, who made much of his personal appearance.

Tom continued to brush the coat collar off with one hand, while unfolding a printed bill with the other. An advertising wagon had gone past the college grounds the day before, and from a fellow distributing handbills Tom had gotten a sheet telling of the merits of "Gumley's Red Pills for Red-Blooded People," and also some small bills relating to the same wonderful cure for many ills. The small sheets were in the books; the large sheet he now proceeded to place on William Philander's back, fastening it under the turned-down coat collar. There were a few specks of talcum powder on the coat collar, but not enough to have attracted any attention.

"Now you are all right, Tubbsky," said the fun-loving Rover. "My, but you certainly do know how to dress!" he added, in affected admiration.

"Ah, really?" lisped the dude. "Thanks.

But please don't knock my books down again," he added, and then proceeded on his way to one of the classrooms.

"Well, that makes me feel a little better," murmured Tom, and then he followed slowly, to watch the fun. He saw a number of students gather and all commenced to snicker at Tubbs, who, totally unconscious of what was taking place, marched on, holding his head erect.

"Wish it was my class, I'd like to see it out," mused Tom. "But never mind, I guess I'll hear about it later," and he turned back to the campus, to wait for Sam. As he did this, a queer pain shot through his head and he murmured a suppressed groan.

"If that keeps on I'll have to do as Sam says, go and see a doctor," he told himself. "Gosh, how queer I feel! Just as if I was getting batty!"

"Hullo, Tom!" came the salute from nearby, and looking in that direction the fun-loving youth saw another student coming up rapidly. "Sam just told me you were going to take a walk and asked me to go along."

"Yes, Songbird, we'll start as soon as Sam gets through with the lesson he's studying. How's the muse these days"

"Oh, I'm not writing much poetry now," answered John Powell, otherwise known as Songbird, because of his efforts at composing verses. "I've got too much to do studying."

"Why don't you write a poem to the professors? Maybe they'd excuse you from recitations for it," and Tom smiled broadly.

"I—er—I did write one little poem about the lessons," answered the would-be poet. "It went like this:

> "The student sat in his room in a chair
> With a look on his face of keen despair;
> Outside his chums were playing ball
> And oft to him they sent a call.
> He wanted to play with all his heart,
> But from his books he could not part."

"Grand! Immense! You've struck the clothespin on the head the first clip!" cried Tom. "Any more of the same brand?"

"Well—er—I started the second verse, but I didn't get it finished. It went like this:

> "He had a lesson hard to learn,
> It made his heart with anguish burn;
> He wanted to throw those books away
> And rush outside and run and play
> And so—and so—and so———"

> "And so he kept on grinding there,
> Gnashing his teeth and pulling his hair,"

finished Tom. "I know, for I've been there. Really, Songbird, that's a dandy poem. You ought to have it framed and hung up in the gym."

"Do you really think so?" and the would-be poet looked pleased.

"I do. It would hit every fellow in Brill. And I think—What can that fellow want?" added Tom suddenly, as a messenger boy from the town came running up to him.

"Guess he's got a message for you," returned Songbird.

"For me? I trust it's no bad news," said Tom.

CHAPTER II

SOMETHING ABOUT THE PAST

"Is this Mr. Thomas Rover?" asked the messenger boy, as he came to a halt.

"Yes, that's my handle," answered Tom. "What have you got for me, a check for a thousand dollars or a bill?"

"Telegram," was the laconic answer, and the lad held it out. "Sign here," he added, bringing his receipt book into evidence. "It's paid fer."

"All right, son." Tom signed the book, fished up a dime from his pocket and handed it to the lad, who took it with a broad grin.

"T'anks, mister. Any answer?"

"I'll see," said Tom, and tore open the envelope of the telegram. He perused the yellow sheet inside with interest.

"It's from Dick!" he cried, to Songbird. "He's got to come to Casford on business and he says he will make the trip in the auto and bring Dora along. They'll be here to-morrow or the day after, and they'll stop at Hope Seminary too. Say, this is great! I must tell Sam!" went on Tom, his face brightening. "You can go," he told the messenger boy.

"Here comes Sam now," announced Songbird. "He's got Stanley and Spud with him." And he pointed to one of the doors of the college building.

To my old readers the Rover boys will need no introduction. For the benefit of others, allow me to state that the youths were three in number, Dick being the oldest, fun-loving Tom coming next, and sturdy little Sam being the youngest. When at "the old homestead," as they called it, they lived with their father, Anderson Rover, and their Uncle Randolph and Aunt Martha on a farm called Valley Brook, in New York State.

As related in the first volume of this series, entitled, "The Rover Boys at School," the three lads had been sent to Putnam Hall Military Academy, a well-known institution of learning presided over by Captain Victor Putnam. There they had made many friends and also a few enemies.*

* For particulars regarding how Putnam Hall Military Academy was organized, and what fine times the cadets there enjoyed even before the Rovers appeared on the scene, read "The Putnam Hall Series," six volumes, starting with "The Putnam Hall Cadets."—PUBLISHERS.

The first term at school was followed by a trip on the ocean, and then another trip into the jungles of Africa. Then came a journey to the West, and jolly times on the Great Lakes and in the mountains. Next the boys returned to the Hall, to go in camp with their fellow cadets. After that they took a long journey over land and sea, being cast away on a lonely island of the Pacific.

"Now I've had enough adventures to last a lifetime," said Dick, on returning home. But strenuous happenings to him and his brothers were not yet over. On a houseboat the Rover boys sailed down the Ohio and the Mississippi rivers, having many adventures by the way, and then found themselves on the Plains, where they solved the mystery of Red Rock ranch. Then they reached Southern Waters, and in the Gulf of Mexico discovered a deserted steam yacht, which they eventually turned over to its anxious owner.

"Now for a good rest," said Sam, and the three lads returned to the home farm, where more adventures befell them. Next they returned to Putnam Hall, where all graduated with considerable honor.

"College next," said Tom, and he made a wry face, for studying was not particularly in his line, although he could knuckle down as hard as anyone when it was necessary. But before they went to college the lads and their father, accompanied by some others, went off on a treasure hunt, locating what was known as the Stanhope fortune.

Brill College was a fine institution of learning, located in the middle west, not far from the town of Ashton. With the Rovers went their old-time school chum, Songbird Powell, already introduced. At the same time William Philander Tubbs came there from Putnam Hall. He was a dudish fellow who thought more of his dress and his personal appearance than anything else, and was often made the butt of some practical joke.

At Brill the Rovers soon made other friends, including Stanley Browne, a tall, gentlemanly youth, and Will Jackson, generally called Spud, because of his unusual fondness for potatoes. Spud was a great story teller and some of his yarns were certainly "the limit," to use Sam's way of expressing it.

While at Putnam Hall the Rover boys had made the acquaintance of Dora Stanhope, who lived nearby with her widowed mother, and also Nellie and Grace Laning, Dora's two cousins. It was not long before Dick and Dora showed a great liking for each other, and at same time Tom commenced to "pair off" with Nellie and Sam was often seen in the company of Grace. Then came the time when the Rovers did a great service for Mrs. Stanhope, saving her from the rascality of Josiah Crabtree, a teacher at Putnam Hall who was trying to get possession of the money Mrs. Stanhope held in trust for Dora. Crabtree was exposed and then he lost no time in disappearing.

Not far from Brill College was located another institution of learning, Hope Seminary, for girls. When the Rovers went to Brill, Dora and her two cousins went to Hope, so the young folks met as often as before.

A short term at Brill was followed by an unexpected trip down East, where the lads again fell in with the rascally Crabtree. Then the youths returned home for a brief vacation and while there became the owners of a biplane and took several thrilling trips through the air, and, later on, by means of the same aircraft, managed to save Dora and Nellie from some rascals who had abducted them.

About this time, Mr. Anderson Rover, who was not well, was having much trouble with some brokers, who were trying to do him out of much valuable property. He went to New York and disappeared, and the sons immediately went in search of him, as related in the volume before this, entitled "The Rover Boys in New York."

The brokers were Pelter, Japson & Company, and it was not long before Dick and his brothers discovered that they were in league with Josiah Crabtree. The plotters were holding Mr. Rover a prisoner, in the hope that he would sign away certain rights to them. The boys traced the crowd to a lonely farmhouse, and it was during the happenings which followed that poor Tom was struck on the head by a wooden footstool, thrown by Pelter, and knocked unconscious. Josiah Crabtree tried to escape from a garret window by means of a rope made of a blanket and this broke and he fell, breaking a leg in two places. He was taken to a hospital and the doctors there said he would be a cripple for life.

All of the Rovers were much concerned over Tom, and for some time it looked as if the youth might be seriously injured. But the boy had grit and pulled himself together, and presently announced himself as well as ever. But he often got that sharp pain through the head, and there were times when, for an instant, his mind became a blank.

While Dick was at college he had become formally engaged to Dora, and now it was decided that, as Mr. Rover was in no physical condition to look after his various financial affairs, and as Dick seemed to take more to business than to studying, he should leave college and take the reins out of his parent's hands. Then he pleaded with Dora that they get married and she consented, only stipulating that they must both look after her mother. Then followed the grandest wedding that quiet Cedarville had ever known, and Dick and Dora went off on a short but exceedingly happy honeymoon trip.

"And now it is back to the college grind for us," Sam had said to Tom.

"Right you are," was the reply. "And we'll have to work pretty hard to catch up with our classes."

"But your head, Tom——"

"Oh, that has got to take care of itself," had been Tom's reply; and there the matter had dropped for the time being. But often Sam would watch his brother closely, for he knew that poor Tom had been seriously hurt and was by no means entirely over it.

When the two brothers had returned to Brill they had had to tell their chums of all their doings in and near New York. Songbird had smiled grimly on hearing of the fate of Josiah Crabtree.

"Well, he deserved it," the would-be poet had said. "He was a snake in the grass from the start."

"I hope he doesn't cross our path again," Sam had replied. "I never want to see him again."

"Nor do I," had come from Tom. "If he's a cripple I reckon he'll keep out of our sight."

It was hard work, after all the excitement of their doings in New York, and the added excitement of the wedding, for Sam and Tom to settle own to the hum-drum routine of life at college, but the lads did their best. Nellie Laning and her sister Grace came back to Hope Seminary and the young folks managed to see each other at least once a week. Nellie was very solicitous about Tom, and when he admitted to her that his head still hurt at times she wanted to know why he didn't return to the farm for a long rest.

"Oh, I don't want to drop behind in my studies, Nellie," had been his answer. "I want to get through, and go into business, like Dick has done," and he gazed at her in a manner that caused her to blush deeply.

"Yes, I know. But, Tom dear, supposing

your head——" She did not know how to go on.

"Oh, my head will be all right, Nellie, so don't you fret. Why, I wouldn't have you fret for the world!" And Tom had caught both her hands tightly within his own. They understood each other perfectly.

"But you know what the doctor said—that you must be very careful for a long, long time." She had not added that one of the specialists had remarked that victims of such injuries sometimes went out of their minds.

"Oh, I'll be all right I tell you, Nellie," he had answered. "I'll go through Brill with a rush, see if I don't. And then we'll get married——"

"Oh, Tom!"

"Surest thing you know," he had added, and then, as they chanced to be alone, he had caught her in his arms and given her a quick little hug and a kiss that meant a great deal. To Tom, the whole world did not hold such another girl like Nellie. And to Nellie—well, there was Tom and that was all.

"Well, you take good care of yourself," she had said on parting, and he had told her again not to worry.

"What's the news?" asked Sam, as he came

up to his brother and saw the telegram in Tom's hand.

"Read it for yourself," was the answer and the younger Rover did so.

"So Dick is coming to Casford, eh?" mused Sam. "I suppose it's some more of Dad's business. Well, I'll be glad to see him and see Dora, too. We can all go up to Hope together."

"Go to Hope to see the teachers, I suppose," said Stanley Browne, closing one eye suggestively. "Fine fun that, seeing the teachers," and then Sam made a playful pass at him with his fist.

"Sam said we were to take a walk," put in Spud. "Where are we going?"

"We might go out towards the Sanderson farm," suggested Songbird.

"So you can call on Minnie," cried Tom, for he knew of Songbird's deep regard for the farmer's daughter. "All right, that suits me."

"Let us go through Lanker's woods and by the old mill," suggested Sam. "That's a fine walk, Tom, and almost as short as the regular road."

"Just as short," put in Songbird. "I've walked it several times and I know." And then he bit his lip as several of the others commenced to laugh. "I don't care—I've got a right to visit the Sandersons if I want to."

"Sure you have," answered Sam. "And Minnie—Great Scott! What's the row now? Here comes Tubbs on the run and shaking his fist at us!"

"I guess I am in for it," returned Tom. "I fancy Tubblets wants to see me."

CHAPTER III

TOM'S JOKE

"WHAT did you do to him?" asked Sam, quickly.

"Put an advertisement of pills on his back and some other ads. in his text books," answered Tom. "Say, he looks some mad; doesn't he?"

"I should say yes," came from Stanley.

William Philander was approaching with long strides. In one hand he held the poster Tom has fastened on his back, and he was shaking his other fist wrathfully.

"Tom Rover, you've—er—insulted me!" he gasped as he came up. "You've humiliated me before the whole class! I'll—I'll——" The dudish student was so full of wrath he could not speak.

"Take a cough drop and clear your throat, Billy," suggested Tom, coolly. "Don't get so excited, you might drop dead from heart disease."

"How dare you put that—er—that advertisement of Gumley's Red Pills on my back?" stormed the stylishly-dressed one.

"'Gumley's Red Pills for Red-Blooded People,'" quoted Spud, from the poster. "Say, they are fine, Willie. Didn't you ever take 'em?"

"No, and I don't want to. I want Tom Ro——"

"Say, if you haven't taken any of Gumley's pills you don't know what you've missed," went on Spud, with a wink at the others. "Why, there was a man over in Rottenberg who was flat on his back with half a dozen fatal diseases. The doctors gave him just three days to live,—three days, think of it! His wife nearly cried her eyes out. Then along came this Gumley man with a trunk full of his Red Pills for Red-Blooded People. He didn't exactly know if the dying man was red-blooded or not, but he took a chance and gave the fellow sixteen pills, four after breakfast, four after dinner, four after supper and four on retiring, and the next day, what do you think happened? That man got up and went to work, and he's been at his job ever since."

"Yes, and not only that," added Tom, earnestly. "That man organized a tug-of-war team,—the plumbers against the Local Conclave of the R. W. Q. Society,—and they've had three tug-of-war matches, and he has pulled the R. W. Q. Society over the line every time. Talk about pills that are worth their weight in gold! Why, Gumley's Red Pills for Red-Blooded People are worth their weight in diamonds, and you ought to get down on your bended knees and thank somebody for having been given the opportunity to advertise them."

"Oh, you make me—er—tired, don't you know," gasped William Philander. "It was a —er—a horrid trick. All the class were laughing at me. And when I opened my Greek book, out fell one of those horrid bills! And then I dropped another bill on the platform, and—oh, it was awful! I'll never forgive you, Tom Rover, never!" And William Philander stalked away, still clutching the poster in his hand.

"Poor William Philander!" murmured Sam. "It was rather a rough joke, Tom."

"Oh, it will do him good," was the answer. "He's too uppish to live."

"Yes, he wants some of the conceit knocked out of him," added Stanley. "But come on, if we are going for a walk, let us get started."

"Wish I had been in the classroom to see the fun," mused Tom, his old-time grin overspreading his face. No matter how old Tom got he'd never give up his boyish pranks.

The crowd of students were soon on the way in the direction of the Sanderson farm. But at the first turn in the road they left that highway, and following a path across a pasture lot, plunged into the depths of what was known as Lanker's woods. Through the woods ran a fair-sized stream of water, and at one spot there was an old dam and the remains of a saw mill, now going to decay.

"Sam, don't you wish you had the old *Dart-away* back," remarked Stanley, presently. "You used to cover this part of the country pretty well with that flying machine?"

"I've never wanted it back since it got smashed up on the railroad track," was the answer. "Flying was good enough, but I don't think I was cut out for a birdman."

"I'd like to go up again some day," put in Tom. "But not regularly. I'd rather travel in an auto, or behind a fast horse."

"Give me a horse every time," said Songbird. And then he warbled softly:

"To rush along at railroad speed,
In auto, or on wings of air,
Is well enough for some, I think,
To make you jump and make you stare.
But when I journey roundabout,
I'll take a horse, or maybe two,
And then I'll—I'll——"

"And then I won't bust any tires
And walk home feeling pretty blue!"

added Tom. "Say, that's right, Songbird, although you can't burst tires on a flying machine," he added.

"That isn't just the way I was going to finish the verse," said the would-be poet. "But it will do."

On went the boys, deeper and deeper into the woods, chatting gaily and occasionally singing snatches of college songs. Sam kept close to his brother and he was glad to note that Tom was acting quite like his old self.

"What he needs is plenty of fresh air and rest from studying," thought the younger Rover. "Hang it all, it was a mistake for Tom to get down to the grind so soon. He ought to have taken a trip out West, or to Europe, or somewhere."

Presently the students came out on the bank of the stream and there, in the sunshine, they rested on a fallen tree and some rocks. It was pleasant to watch the swiftly-rushing water, as it tumbled over the stones.

"The brook is pretty strong on account of those rains we had," remarked Sam.

Yes, I never saw it so swift," answered Stanley.

"Humph! this is nothing," announced Spud. "I saw it once when it ran so swiftly that the water couldn't make the turn at the bend below here and ran right up the hill and over on Shelby's barn, drowning sixteen cows! And some of the water hit the barn roof and bounced off into the chimney of Shelby's cottage and put out the fire, and——"

"Wow, Spud! put on the soft pedal!" interrupted Sam.

"Oh, it's absolutely true. Some day I'll show you the tombstone they erected over the sixteen cows. It's of granite and a hundred and ten feet high."

"Never mind the tombstone," interrupted Tom. "What I want to see is the match box Shelby stored that water in after it hit the barn." And at this sally a general laugh went up.

On the boys went again, and half an hour later reached the abandoned saw mill. All that was left was the dam with the broken wheel and one end of what had once been a long, low, one-storied building.

"Let's have a look inside," suggested Stanley, and led the way, and the others followed. Sam was the last to enter, coming directly behind his brother and he saw Tom suddenly put his hand to the back of his head and stop.

"Does it hurt again, Tom?" he whispered, kindly.

"Just a—a—spasm!" gasped poor Tom, and then he drew a long breath. "There, it's gone now," he added, and walked on. Sam sighed and shook his head. What was this queer condition of Tom going to lead to? It made him shiver to think of it.

There was but little to see in the old mill. It was a damp, unwholesome place, and the boys soon came out again. Not far away was a well hole, rather deep and partly filled with water.

Tom was the first to notice this hole, which was partly covered with rotted boards. Of a sudden he commenced to grin, as if he scented a huge joke. He ran up and rearranged the rotted boards, so they completely covered the hole. Then in the center he placed the bright-colored cap he had been wearing, and hurried along, to the path leading beside the dam.

"Hi, Stanley!" he called out, as the others came from the mill. "Get my cap, will you? The wind blew it off. It's back there somewhere."

"I see it!" shouted Stanley.

"I see it, too," came from Spud, who was close by. "I'll race you for it, Stan."

"Done!" was the reply, and side by side the two collegians raced for the cap.

"An apple for the fellow who wins!" shouted Sam, who saw nothing wrong in what was going on.

"Leg it, both of you!" added Songbird.

Side by side Stanley and Spud sped over the uneven ground in the direction of the cap. Then both made a plunge forward in true football style. In a heap they landed on the rotted boards, each catching hold of the coveted headwear. Then came an ominous crash, and both boys disappeared headlong into the well hole!

"Look! Look what has happened!" shrieked Sam, in dismay.

"They are in the old well!" gasped Songbird.

"Ha! ha! ha! Ho! ho!" came from Tom, and he shook with laughter. "Isn't that the dandy joke? I thought Stanley would go in, but I didn't expect to catch the pair of 'em."

"Tom!" cried Sam, in new horror. "You didn't really mean——"

"Sure I did. I put my cap there on purpose. Say, they had some tumble, didn't they?" And Tom commenced to laugh again—a strange laugh that didn't sound like him at all.

"They'll be drowned—we must save them!" exclaimed Sam, hoarsely. "Songbird, what can we do?" he added, turning to his chum.

"I don't know—maybe we can throw 'em a rope—if there is one around."

"Let 'em crawl out—it's easy enough," came from Tom. "Don't you spoil the joke." And he commenced to laugh again.

"Tom, don't act as if you were crazy!" said Sam, catching him by the arm and shaking him. "Those fellows can't get out without help—it's too deep! And the sides may cave in on top of them! And there is water down there, too! We must help them, and at once."

Tom stared at his brother in bewilderment. Then of a sudden the look of fun died out of his face and was succeeded by a look of horror and terror combined.

"Did I do that, Sam? Oh, what a foolish thing to do! Yes, we must help them! What shall I do? I'll jump down after them if you say so!" And Tom started forward.

"No, don't do that!" Sam held him back. "We'll get a rope, or a long pole. Don't go too close or you may cave the top of the well in on 'em."

"Yes, we must get a rope, or a pole," gasped poor Tom and ran off on a search. "And I thought I was having a good joke! Oh, I certainly must be going crazy!" he muttered.

In the meantime Songbird had thrown himself on his hands and knees and crawled to the edge of the old well hole. He called out several times, but got no reply. He heard a great floundering and splashing.

"Hi, you!" he continued. "Are you alive?"

"Sa—save us!" came the spluttered-out words, from Spud. "Sa—save us!"

"Are you both alive?" continued Songbird, anxiously.

"Yes," answered Stanley. "But we need help, for the water is over our heads. Get a rope, or something, and be quick about it!"

"Hang on the best you can and we'll help you," was the answer.

"Well, don't be too long about it, or we'll be drowned!" came in a shivering tone from Spud.

CHAPTER IV

THE OLD WELL HOLE

THE three youths at the top of the old well hole gazed around anxiously. All were looking for a rope, but no such article presented itself to their view. There was a bit of iron chain lying in the dead leaves nearby, but it was too short to be of service.

"I don't see anything to use," remarked Songbird, wildly. "Oh, Sam, this is awful!"

"Come on, I think I see something," answered the younger Rover. "Tom, you can help bring it over."

He took his half-dazed brother by the arm, more to keep him from approaching too close to the well than for any other reason, and the three boys raced to where a number of saplings were growing. Sam had noted that one of the saplings had been bent over by the wind and was partly uprooted.

"Maybe we can get it up—we've got to do

it!" he cried. "Come, catch hold and pull for all you are worth!"

The others understood and laid hold of the young tree, which was all of fifteen feet high and several inches in diameter. It had but few branches, which was an advantage. They bent it down and pulled with a will, and out of the ground it came, so suddenly that the boys fell flat on their backs.

"Wait, I'll break off some of the branches!" cried Sam. "Tom, Songbird, try to break off that twisted root. There, that will do. Now, if we can get it down the well they ought to be able to climb up on it."

It was but the work of a few seconds to drag the sapling to the hole. Then it was lifted upright, so that the end might not dig into the sides of the well and cause a cave-in.

"Look out below there!" shouted Sam.

"Don't knock any stones on us!" came back from Stanley. He and Spud had braced themselves on the sides of the old well, with the water up to their waists.

"We'll be as careful as we can," answered Songbird.

"Look out for dirt in your eyes," added Tom. All the fun had died out of him and his face was full of concern.

Slowly and cautiously the three boys lowered the sapling into the old well hole. In doing this they had to stand close to the edge, and once they sent down a shower of loose dirt that caused a wild cry of alarm from below.

"Go slow!" cried Spud, presently. "I've got it," he added, a second later. "Let her come," and then the sapling was lowered until the roots rested on the bottom of the hole. The top was now several feet below the top of the old well.

"The old chain—just the thing!" cried Sam, and took it up.

"You had better come up close together," suggested Songbird, peering down at those below. "Then, if the well caves in, you'll be up that far anyway."

This was thought good advice and Stanley and Spud determined to act on it. Stanley came first with Spud at his heels. The many small branches of the sapling afforded good holds, and as each of the youths was something of an athlete, both of them came up with comparative ease.

"Can't get any higher," remarked Stanley, when within two feet of the top of the sapling. "It's almost ready to break now."

"Catch hold of the chain!" cried Sam. "I'll

hold it. Tom and Songbird, you hold me, so I don't fall in."

Sam had the chain twisted around his right hand and he leaned far over into the well hole, his brother and Songbird holding him by his free arm. The loose end of the chain dangled close to Stanley and he grasped hold. Then came a short, hard pull, and Stanley came sprawling out on the grass. Then Spud crawled up a little higher and he was hauled out the same way.

Both boys were wet to the skin and covered with mud, presenting anything but an enviable appearance. For several seconds they sat on the grass, panting for breath.

"Phew! that was a close shave!" gasped Spud, presently. "I'm mightily glad the old well didn't cave in on us!"

"We went down head first," came from Stanley. "If it hadn't been for the water we would have smashed our skulls!"

"And the water came close to drowning us," added Spud. "And say, it was some cold, believe me," and he shivered.

"You'd better race around in the sun a bit, or you'll take cold," said Sam.

"Take off your coat, Spud, and put on mine," said Songbird, as he commenced to divest himself of his garment.

"Yes, and Stanley can have my coat," came from Tom. He now looked relieved, but his eyes had a strange light in them.

"It's queer how your old cap landed right on the top of the well," remarked Spud. "Why didn't the wind carry it to some safer place?"

At this remark Tom's face grew suddenly red. He tried to speak and gave a gulp.

"There isn't much wind now," added Stanley. "How was it, Tom?"

"I—er—I—the wind didn't blow the cap," was the lame answer. Just then Tom wished he was a thousand miles away. He could not look his chums in the face.

"It didn't blow the cap?" demanded Spud. "What do you mean?"

To this Tom did not answer. Sam wanted to speak, but did not know what to say. Songbird looked curiously at Tom.

"Say, look here!" burst out Stanley, striding forward. "Do you mean to say, Tom Rover, that you put that cap on the old well on purpose?"

"I—I—did," answered Tom feebly. "I—er—I thought it was a—a joke."

"A joke!" cried Spud, sarcastically.

"A joke, to put us in peril of drowning, or

smothering to death!" roared Stanley. "If you call that a joke I don't, and I want you to know it!" And in a sudden passion he doubled up his fists and sprang towards Tom.

But Sam rushed between the pair.

"Stanley, don't, please don't!" he cried. "Tom made a mistake,—he knows it now."

"He'll know it after I am done with him!" cried the other, hotly. "He's not going to play a joke on me that puts me in danger of my life! I'll take it out of his hide!" And he tried to get past the younger Rover.

But still Sam held him back.

"Stanley, don't touch him. You know how sick he's been. He isn't himself. Let it pass. He's as sorry as any of us that it happened; aren't you, Tom?"

"Sure I am," answered Tom, readily; but his tone of voice was that of one who didn't care much, one way or the other. Tom was not himself, that was certain.

"Humph, maybe he's sorry and maybe he isn't," muttered Stanley. "I guess he ought to have a thrashing. Anyway, I am done with him," and he flung back the coat Tom had offered him.

All in the crowd looked at Tom, expecting

him to say something more. But Tom shut his mouth tightly and walked away, up the river path. He was without his coat. Sam picked up the garment and made after his brother.

"Tom, come back here!"

"I won't, Sam. You can stay with them if you want to. I'll take a walk alone," was the moody answer, and Tom walked faster than ever.

"Of all the mean things to do!" murmured Spud, shaking his head slowly. "I would never have thought it of Tom Rover, never!"

"Tom hasn't acted just right since he came back to Brill," said Songbird, in a low tone. "You know he got an awful crack on the head, and, somehow, he's been different ever since. I wouldn't lay it up against him, if I were you fellows."

"Huh! I guess you'd lay it up against him if you had been soused down into that old well hole and were all wet and covered with mud!" growled Stanley. "Fun is fun, but that was no joke, I can tell you that! He deserves a good thrashing."

"If he isn't right in his head they ought to put him under the doctor's care, or in a sanitarium," remarked Spud. "Why, if he isn't right in his mind there is no telling what he'll do next! He might take it into his head to murder some of us!"

"Oh, I don't think it's as bad as that," answered Songbird, hastily. "I think in a short while he'll be just as he used to be. But the excitement of that capture of those brokers and old Crabtree, and the fight, and then Dick's wedding, were too much for him. What he needs, I think, is a good, long rest."

"Well, he can keep away from me after this," grumbled Stanley, as he looked at his wet and bedrabbled clothes. "Nice sight we'll present going back to the college!"

"I'll tell you what I'll do," suggested Songbird. "I'll go ahead, to the gym., and get you some changes and you can put them on in Dobb's barn. Then nobody will know about it."

"All right," said Stanley, his face brightening a trifle.

"What of Sam and Tom?" asked Spud, who was not as angry as his companion in misfortune.

"I'll tell them we are going back," answered Songbird, and ran after the Rovers.

In the meantime Sam and Tom had kept on walking—or rather Tom had hurried on and his brother had kept up with him, trying to make him turn back. But to all of Sam's entreaties Tom turned a deaf ear.

"I came out for a walk and I'm going to walk," he said, stubbornly. "If they want to go back they can do it—and you and Songbird can go with 'em."

"But, Tom, that isn't fair," insisted Sam. "They are all wet, and——"

"Humph! a little water won't hurt 'em. I've been soaked myself more than once. If they can't take a joke let 'em go," and Tom continued to stalk on until he came to a flat rock, when he suddenly sat down to rest, at the same time putting both hands to his head.

It was here that Songbird found them and informed them of what the others and himself proposed to do.

"All right, Songbird; I guess that is best," said Sam, softly. "Tom doesn't feel just right and he'll rest here awhile."

"Oh, I'm not sick!" cried Tom. "I'm sorry I played the trick, but I don't see any reason for Stanley and Spud to cut up about it." And then he got up as suddenly as he had sat down and stalked on once more.

"Do your best to fix it up, Songbird," pleaded Sam, in a low tone. "You can see Tom isn't himself. Try to explain to those fellows."

"I will. I think Tom ought to have a doctor," was the low reply; and then Songbird rejoined Stanley and Spud and the three started back to Brill.

Tom stalked on for fully half a mile without speaking and Sam came behind him. The younger Rover was busy thinking and did not say a word. Presently the pair reached the end of the river path and came to a bridge and the highway. On the bridge Tom sat down again.

"Want to go any further, Tom?" asked Sam, as pleasantly as he could.

"I don't care where I go!" burst out the other. "I'm sick of it all! Sick of the college, sick of studying, sick of those fellows, sick of everything and everybody! I wish I could go to Africa, or the North Pole, or somewhere else, where I wouldn't see or hear of 'em again!"

"Tom!"

"I mean it. What's the use of keeping in the grind day after day, like a horse on a tread mill? What does a fellow get out of it? Nothing but hard work and a pain in the head! Some times my head hurts to beat the band! I can't stand it, and I won't! They are all against me, every one of 'em!" And Tom commenced to wring his hands, while two tears stood in his eyes and rolled down his cheeks.

CHAPTER V

TOM'S QUEER ACTIONS

SAM did not know what to say or what to do. He realized more fully than ever that his brother was not himself. He was growing wilder and more irrational every moment.

"Tom," he asked suddenly, "have you got those pills with you that the doctor gave you to take?"

"Sure," was the ready answer.

"Have you taken any lately?"

"No. What's the use? They don't seem to help me."

"Let me see them, please."

"There they are." Tom brought the box from his pocket. "They might as well be bread pills, or Gumley's red ones," and he grinned for a moment at the recollection of the trick played on William Philander Tubbs.

Sam took the box and looked at the directions carefully. "It says to take one three times a day when needed," he said. "You had better take one now, Tom. Come on."

"It won't do any good, Sam."

"Well, take one for me, that's a good fellow. Wait, I've got my pocket cup and I'll get some water." And he did so.

"Oh, dear, you're bound to feed me pills," sighed Tom, and made a wry face as he swallowed the one Sam handed him. Sam kept the box, making up his mind that he would play nurse after this.

"I guess we had better walk some more," said Tom, suddenly. "I hate sitting still. If we had the old *Dartaway* I'd take a sail from here to San Francisco, or some other far-off place."

"Wait a little, I'm tired," answered Sam, soothingly. "Just see those little fishes!" he said, pointing to the water under the bridge.

He made Tom get down and watch the fishes and bathed his brother's forehead. At first Tom was rather restless, but soon the pill seemed to take effect and he grew quiet.

"I'm getting awfully tired," he announced, presently. "I guess we had better be getting back, Sam."

"Just as you say, Tom," was the quiet reply.

It was growing dark when they reached the college grounds and most of the students had gone in to supper. Tom said he did not feel much like eating, but his brother told him he had better have a little food, and they went in together. They saw Songbird and the others at another table. The would-be poet and Spud nodded to them, but Stanley paid no attention.

Sam and Tom still occupied their old room, Number 25, while Songbird was still in Number 26. Since Dick was not to return to Brill his place in the latter room had been taken by Max Spangler, a jolly fellow of German-American parentage.

"Vot is der madder mit Dom Rofer?" asked Max of the would-be poet, as both came up to the room after supper.

"Oh, he isn't feeling very well, Max," was the reply. "What makes you ask?"

"Oh, I see him put his hands by his head on so many dimes," said Max. "He got knocked owit, didn't he?"

"Yes, a rascal hit him over the head with a wooden footstool and nearly cracked his skull."

"Den he should be py der hospital, yah, instead of py college," said the German-American student.

"Well, maybe they'll have to take him to the hospital, or somewhere," returned Songbird, thoughtfully. "Hang it all, with Dick gone and Tom acting as he does, times are not half as jolly as they used to be!"

In the next room Sam sat down to study. Tom had wanted to study, too, but his brother had persuaded him to lie down and rest, and now he was asleep and breathing heavily. Sam tiptoed his way across the room to gaze at him.

"Poor, poor Tom!" he murmured softly. "He'll have to take it easy. If he tries to keep up here it may kill him, or——" Sam did not finish. It was a terrorizing thought to imagine that Tom might go out of his mind. "He's got to have a doctor—some specialist. I'm glad Dick is coming, so we can talk it over. But it's too bad to burden Dick with this—and Dora, too—when they aren't over their honeymoon yet. Oh, dear, it's too bad Pelter threw that footstool at Tom!"

Tom continued to sleep and Sam tried his best to study. But it was hard work and the youngest Rover made slow progress. An hour passed and then there came a soft tap on the door. Songbird was there.

"I thought I'd ask how he was," he whispered, nodding towards Tom.

"Sound asleep, Songbird." Sam paused for a moment. "Come in," and his chum did so, and Sam closed the door again. "I wanted to ask you about Stanley and Spud."

"I—I tried to explain to them, without going

into it too deeply," said Songbird. "I think Spud understands. But Stanley — well, he's pretty well riled yet. But I guess he'll get over it."

"You can tell 'em that Tom would never play such a trick if he was—well just right here," and Sam touched his forehead. "It's an awful state of affairs, Songbird! I hardly know what to do."

"Why not send Tom home for a rest?"

"How can I if he won't go?"

"Get the doctor to order it."

"That's an idea. I'll talk it over with Dick when he comes. But I wish you could fix it up with Stanley."

"I'll do my best," answered Songbird, and then, as Tom moved restlessly, he hastily left the room as quietly as he had entered it.

Before Sam went to bed Tom roused up and wanted a drink of water. His brother made him take another of the pills and then both retired. For a long time Sam could not sleep, but at last he fell into a profound slumber.

When Sam awoke it was with a start, for the sun was shining brightly and he feared he had overslept himself. He glanced to where Tom had been resting and uttered an exclamation.

"Gone! I wonder where he went to?"

He glanced at the chair on which Tom had placed his clothes and saw that it was empty. The door to the corridor was ajar.

"Can he have been walking in his sleep, or did he wander away out of his mind?" was the agonizing thought that rushed through Sam's mind. In a jiffy he was out of bed and had begun to dress. He did not spend longer than was necessary on his toilet. Then he hurried out of the room and gazed about him. An assistant janitor was nearby, running a vacuum cleaner over the floor.

"Gilson, you know my brother Tom," he said. "Have you seen him?"

"Saw him outside quite a while ago," was the reply.

"Where did he go?"

"I don't know. He was near the gym."

"Thanks."

It did not take Sam long to reach the campus. Fully a score of Brill students were in evidence, but a quick glance showed that Tom was not among them.

"Hello, Sam!" came from Bob Grimes, one of the crowd. "How goes it this morning?"

"Fine, Bob. Have you seen Tom?"

"Yes, he took a walk down the road."

"Which way?"

"Towards town."

"Long ago?"

"Best part of half an hour, I guess."

Sam said no more but hurried across the broad campus and on to the highway leading to Ashton. The big bell in the tower was sending out its last call for breakfast. Sam put down the road on a run, all sorts of thoughts wandering through his brain. What if Tom was clean out of his mind and had wandered off?

"Whoop! Sam! Where bound in such a hurry, child?" came the unexpected call from a nearby field, and Tom vaulted the rail fence lightly. "Taking the morning air, like myself?"

"Tom!" gasped the younger brother, coming to a halt. He ran up closer and gave the other a quick look. Tom's eyes were as bright as they had ever been. "Are you feeling all right this morning?" he faltered.

"Best I've felt in a long time, Sam. Say, were you coming after me?" demanded Tom, quickly.

"Yes, if you want to know."

"Thought I was going to run away, eh? Well, you're mistaken, Sammy, my son. I'm not going to do anything of the sort. You know how bad I felt yesterday."

"You certainly were bad yesterday. But come on, it's time for breakfast."

"All right, Sam," and the two walked to the college side by side. "Say, I did some queer things yesterday, didn't I?" went on the fun-loving Rover, anxiously.

"You certainly did, Tom."

"Got Spud and Stanley in a regular mess."

"Worse than that. They were in danger of their lives."

"I was a fool, Sam, a regular, downright fool, and I'll tell 'em so when I get a chance. But it was my head,—it wasn't just right."

"You must take another pill, Tom. Here it is, take it as soon as you can get some water."

"All right, Sam, you're the doctor and what you say goes. I certainly don't want to act like I did yesterday again," and poor Tom looked greatly worried.

"It's that crack you got on the head, Tom. You want to go slow with studying and with all excitement. Maybe you had better go back home and take it easy."

"Well, I will if I don't feel stronger in a week or two," was the slow and thoughtful answer. And then Tom put his hand to the back of his head, as he had done so many times lately.

It was not until the noon hour that the fun-loving Rover had a chance to talk to Spud and Stanley. He went up to both of his chums frankly and told them what he had told Sam.

"Oh, it's all right," said Spud, quickly. "I knew you weren't yourself, Tom. Don't say anything more about it."

With Stanley, however, it was different. He had spoiled a good suit of clothing and scratched his chin and hands. Sam had told him to send the suit to the cleaner's at the Rovers' expense, but even this had not altogether satisfied the big student.

"It was a mean joke, and I don't like it," said Stanley. "It was no sort of thing to do at all, Tom Rover. If you are going to act like that in the future I don't want anything to do with you," and he left Tom standing helplessly where the two had met. Then Tom rejoined Sam, feeling as uncomfortable as ever.

"I suppose it is all right, Tom," said his younger brother.

"It's all right as far as Spud is concerned," was the moody reply.

"What about Stanley, didn't you speak to him?"

"I did, but he is as mad as hops. He said if I was going to play that kind of jokes he didn't want anything to do with me," and Tom sank in an easy chair in the room. "Sam, I guess I put my foot in it that time. Stanley is a fine fellow and if he talks like that he's got a reason for it."

"He doesn't understand the situation, Tom. I'll speak to him as soon as I get a chance."

"No, don't do it. I told him how it was, but he won't believe it. And why should he? I'm all right, am I not? I'm not crazy, or anything like that, am I?" and Tom looked at his brother pleadingly. "I ought to know what I am doing."

"Of course you are not crazy, Tom. Nobody said you were. That crack on the head put you—well, a little out of sorts, that's all."

"If I thought I was going crazy, I'd—I'd—well I guess I'd jump overboard," said Tom, and he heaved a deep sigh. Then he very abruptly turned to the table, got out one of his text books, and commenced to study.

CHAPTER VI

BOYS AND GIRLS

"HURRAH, Tom! Here's good news!"

"From Dick and Dora?"

"Yes. They will be here at half-past two. Dick stopped to transact that business first, so he and Dora can spend the rest of the time with us and with the girls at Hope. Isn't that just fine?" And Sam's face showed his pleasure.

"All to the merry," was Tom's comment. "Say, I guess we can all go over to Hope together, can't we?" he asked anxiously.

"We'll make a try for it anyway," returned his brother.

It was the day after the events recorded in the last chapter, and Tom had declared in the morning that he felt better than ever. He had even gone out on the campus to joke with Songbird and William Philander Tubbs, and speak a few words with Spud. Stanley had seen him and kept out of his way, and that was the only cloud on the horizon.

"I've got nothing on to-day after two o'clock," went on Tom, with a grin. "How about you?"

"I've got a physics lecture, but I guess I can cut it," answered Sam. "I'll get Spud to tell me all about it afterwards. I wouldn't miss the chance to go to Hope for anything."

They had heard from Dick early in the morning by telegram, and now had come in a message over the long-distance telephone. The oldest Rover brother and his bride were making the tour in the Rover family car, doing this for the express purpose of giving the others a ride when they stopped at Brill and Hope. Dick of course wanted to see all the boys at the college and Dora was equally anxious to visit with the girls at the seminary.

Promptly on time the shrill tone of an auto horn was heard, and Tom and Sam ran across the campus to greet the new arrivals. Dick was at the wheel and Dora sat beside him, smiling and blushing prettily. In the tonneau of the big car rested several bags and wraps.

"Welcome to our city!" sang out Tom, gaily. "And how is Mrs. Rover this afternoon?" and he made a profound bow and swept the ground with his cap.

"The same old Tom, I see!" cried Dora

gaily. "Are you feeling all right?" she asked, quickly.

"Sure," was the answer. Tom was the last one to put on a doleful face in front of a lady.

"Talk about style," came from Sam, merrily. "Nothing like keeping the Rover name up!" And he leaped on the running board and shook hands. "Did you have a good trip?"

"Fine. Not a puncture," answered Dick.

"Oh, it was just too lovely for anything!" cried Dora. "If Dick had the time I'd like to go on a tour for a month!"

"I thought maybe you fellows would like to get in and run over to Hope," went on Dick, with a smile.

"You couldn't keep us out," answered Tom, promptly.

"We telephoned for them to be ready for us," said Dora. "But you will have to take our baggage out, to make room."

"Here comes Songbird, he'll look after that, I know he will," said Sam.

The would-be poet came up all smiles and shook hands. He said he would do anything they wished and at once took charge of the things. Several others came up, including Spud and Stanley, and there was a general handshaking and a rapid-fire of conversation. Then Sam and Tom got in the automobile and away went the car in the direction of Hope Seminary.

"Want me to drive?" asked Tom.

"Tom, you'd better sit in the back with me," put in Sam, quickly. "This is Dick's outing, let him run the car." He was afraid that if Tom got his hands on the wheel he might do something to put the crowd in danger.

"All right, I'm satisfied," was the ready answer and Tom sank back on the cushions.

The touring car was a powerful one and Dick knew how to handle it to perfection. Along the smooth road they rolled swiftly, only slowing down at the turns and where the highway was not in a good state of repair. Dora turned around to talk to the others, asking about the college, and then spoke about those left at Cedarville and at Valley Brook.

"Mamma is real well again," she said. "Better, in fact, than she has been in a long while. I know she feels relieved to think that Dick can now take charge of all of her affairs, and of my affairs, too."

"Dick is getting to be a business man fast," remarked Sam. "With your affairs and Dad's affairs he must be having his hands full."

"Oh, the more the merrier," answered the

oldest brother. "I like it better than going to college." But as he spoke his face became very thoughtful. Clearly Dick had something on his mind. He was not nearly as talkative as usual, Sam soon noticed that and so did Tom.

Presently the touring car came in sight of Hope Seminary, nestling in a pretty grove of trees. Two girls were down by the stone gateway, and both waved their hands.

"Grace and Nellie!"

"Here they come!"

"I told you they'd bring Sam and Tom."

"Doesn't Dora look sweet in that brown suit!"

"And how handsome Dick is getting!"

"Say, Tom looks awfully pale." These words came from Nellie, and as she spoke she turned a bit pale herself.

"To be sure—he's been real sick," answered Grace. "But he'll soon get over it, don't worry," she added, trying to comfort her sister.

By this time the touring car had come to a halt, and Dora and Dick and the two college boys were getting out. Then followed more handshaking and not a few kisses. Dora hugged her cousins and was hugged in return. All felt very happy and their faces showed it.

Of course Dick and Dora had to tell all about

the trip, how they had gotten on the wrong road, and how a drove of cows had once blocked their way, and how they had stopped at one hotel where they had heard a concert given for charity.

"And the weather has been almost ideal," said Dick. "Only one little shower that was just enough to lay the dust on the roads that weren't oiled."

To give Tom and Sam a chance to "visit" with Nellie and Grace, Dick continued to run the car, with Dora at his side, and all of the others in the back. With Nellie near him, Tom seemed to brighten up considerably and told a number of jokes that made everybody laugh. But with it all, he was by no means as lively as was natural with him.

"I've got it all arranged to go to Spotswood," said Dick. "I telephoned to the big hotel there to have a table ready for us. And we'll come back in the moonlight."

"Oh glorious moonlight!" returned Sam, and gave Grace a look that caused her to blush deeply.

"Say, let us sing one of the old time songs!" cried Tom, and started one that had been their favorite ever since going to Putnam Hall Military Academy.

"That's like old times!" exclaimed Dick.

"But please don't sing so loud or you may scare the car," and this sally caused a general laugh.

"Don't you miss the seminary, Dora?" asked Nellie.

"Of course I do, but—but——"

"She'd rather be with Dick," finished Sam, with a wink.

"To be sure I would, Mr. Smarty," came promptly from the bride.

"Wish I could leave college, as Dick did," put in Tom, with a glance at Nellie. "I hate books anyway."

"Oh, that's because you are not strong yet, Tom," said Dora, sympathetically.

"I've told him he ought to take more of a rest," said Sam.

"Oh, let's talk about something else," cried Tom. "I'm tired of being held up as an object of sympathy. Look at the little calf!" he continued, pointing to a field beside the roadway. "A fellow could pick it up in his arms. Say, wouldn't it be great to introduce that calf in Professor Blackie's bedroom some night."

"No more such tricks, Tom!" answered Dick, almost sternly. "You've got to settle down."

"Oh, must I, Papa?" returned Tom, in a trembling childish treble. "Yes, Papa, I'll be your own little good boy." And then another general laugh went up.

"We hardly have any fun any more at Hope," said Nellie. "It's just lessons and lectures from morning to night, and the instructors are that sharp! Yesterday I missed a question in ancient history and I was nearly scared to death."

"Humph! ancient history is enough to scare anybody to death. What's the use of studying ancient history when there is so much history still to come of which we know absolutely nothing?" and Tom looked around with the air of a profound professor.

"Here is where we once came over in the *Dartaway,*" said Dick, a little later. "I guess you'll remember that ride," he added, to his bride.

"Shall I ever forget it!" murmured Dora. "Oh, how glad I was to get away from that horrid Josiah Crabtree and those Sobbers!" went on the girl, with a shudder. She referred to a happening which has been related in detail in "The Rover Boys in the Air."

"Well, the Sobbers are going to get what is coming to them," put in Tom.

"And old Crabtree, too," said Dick. "They told me up at the hospital that the double break in his leg will make him more or less of a cripple for life."

"Well, if ever a man deserved to be punished it was Josiah Crabtree," said Sam. "He was a bad egg from the first time we met him at Putnam Hall. But I say, let us forget all that unpleasant past and enjoy ourselves," and he started up another song, and the others joined in.

By six o'clock they reached Spotswood and Dick ran the touring car around to the big hotel located there. Then they went inside and washed up a little. In the dining room a special table had been set for them in an alcove. There was a big bouquet in the center and a small bouquet at each plate.

"Say, Dick, this is immense!" said Sam, admiringly.

"Just too lovely for anything!" burst out the Laning girls simultaneously.

"How did you come to think of the flowers?" asked Tom, putting his bouquet in his buttonhole and letting Nellie pin it fast.

"That was Dora's idea," answered the big brother.

"I thought it would brighten things up," said Dora. "It's our first dinner together since—since—you know," and she blushed prettily.

"Since the wedding feast," said Sam. "Well, it's just A, Number One! Couldn't be better!"

"That's what!" cried Tom.

Dick and Dora had ordered the dinner with care, so there was a well-selected course, starting with tomato bisque soup and ending with ice-cream and crackers, cheese and coffee. They had some dainty fish and an extra tenderloin steak, and it is perhaps needless to state that the boys did full justice to all that was set before them, and the girls also ate heartily, for all were still in their growing years. Tom created some fun by sticking some stalks of celery in the big center bouquet on the sly and then asking Dora what sort of flowers she had ordered mixed in. And Nellie told Dick he ought to make a speech and he said he'd leave that to Tom, whereupon the irrepressible Tom said he would deliver a lecture on 'How to Cook for Two Alone' if Dick and Dora wanted to listen. Then the fun became general and lasted long after the meal was over.

It was moonlight outside and presently all went to the broad veranda of the hotel. Tom naturally paired off with Nellie and Sam with Grace, and Dick and Dora wisely kept out of the way.

"We had our day, now let them have theirs," said Dick, to his bride.

"By all means, Dick," returned Dora, with a smile that made him pinch her arm. "But listen, dear," she added, in a whisper. "Did you—did you notice Tom?"

"Yes."

"He tries to keep up, but he isn't himself at all."

"I know it, and so does Sam, and, I might as well admit it, Dora, both of us are a good deal worried," replied the young husband, gravely.

CHAPTER VII

COLLEGE DAYS

Sam and Grace sat in a corner of the piazza for the best part of half an hour, and during that time the girl told of her various doings at Hope and about the news from home, and Sam related what had occurred at Brill, omitting, however, to tell how Tom had sent Spud and Stanley into the old well hole. There was a good deal of nonsense added to the conversation, and it must be admitted that Sam held Grace's hand as much as she would permit. They also spoke about the wedding of Dick and Dora, and of the good times they had enjoyed on that occasion.

Tom and Nellie took a stroll through a little park opposite the hotel. What they talked about none of the others knew at the time, but Nellie came back looking very sober and thoughtful, so that her sister wondered if Tom had really and truly proposed to her. Tom was whistling softly to himself, as if to keep up his courage.

"Well, I guess it is time to start on the return, if you young ladies have got to be in by ten," said Dick, at last. "Even as it is I haven't allowed any time for punctures or breakdowns."

"Perish the thoughts of such happenings!" cried Grace.

"We've had our blow-out where I like it best —at the hotel," added Sam, and this joke caused a smile.

As before, Dick drove the car, with Dora beside him, and the others in the tonneau. He had all his lights lit, making the roadway almost as bright as day. Once out of town, the oldest Rover put on speed until they were flying along grandly.

"Oh, Dick, be careful!" pleaded Dora. "You might hit something in the dark."

"Not much to hit on this road," he answered. "But I'll look out, don't fear."

"Oh, let her go!" shouted Tom, recklessly. "Why, you can get ten miles more of speed, Dick, if you try. Let her out for all you are worth!"

"Oh, Tom!" pleaded Nellie, and as he arose and waved his hand she pulled him down on the seat. "If you don't look out you'll fall out."

"'Look out, fall out!'" repeated Tom. "A good joke! Ha! ha! Let her out, Dick!" And he tried to stand up again. "Want me to help?" And he leaned over his brother's shoulder and took hold of the steering wheel.

"Drop it, Tom!" exclaimed Dick, warningly. "Do you want to steer us into a ditch? Drop it, I say!" And he pushed Tom with his elbow.

"Sit down, Tom," called Sam, and caught hold of his brother. "Don't monkey like that in the dark,—it's dangerous."

"Oh, I was only fooling," returned the fun-loving one. "Can't you stand for a little sport?" and then he sank in a corner and had nothing more to say for some time. Nellie heaved a deep sigh and for a moment buried her face in her hands.

All too soon Hope Seminary was reached and Sam and Tom escorted the Laning girls to the doorway of that institution. There was a fond good night, cut somewhat short on Nellie's part, and then the Rover boys returned to the touring car.

"What a grand time," murmured Grace, as she and her sister went upstairs to the room they occupied.

"Was it?" asked Nellie, absently. "I am glad you enjoyed it."

"Why, Nellie, didn't you?"

"No."

"Oh!" And Grace clutched her sister by the arm. "What do you mean?"

"I—I can't tell you!" burst out the other, and then she fairly ran for their room, and, once inside, threw herself on her bed and burst into tears. Grace came after her, locked the door, and sat down and held her hand. She thought she understood and determined to ask no more questions.

"You are going to stay in Ashton over night, are you not?" questioned Sam, of his brother, as the auto neared Brill.

"Yes."

"I want to see you—to talk about Dad's affairs,—and about Tom," went on the youngest Rover, in a whisper.

"All right, Sam. I'll get up early and run over here before breakfast. I'll be at the gate at seven o'clock—if it is clear. I'll see you first and then talk to Tom;" and so it was arranged.

"Here, what's the secret?" demanded Tom, abruptly.

"Nothing much," answered Sam. "Dick will be over to see us in the morning, before he and Dora go back."

"Oh, all right." Tom gave a sudden chuckle.

"Wish I had brought that calf along. I could have a barrel of fun with him to-night!"

"You're going right to bed, and so am I," answered Sam. "We've had fun enough for the present." And then he and his brother said good-bye to Dora, for they did not expect to see her again for some time to come.

Sam was afraid that Tom might not want to go to bed so soon, but his fears were groundless. Tom undressed at once and inside of five minutes was in profound slumber. He occasionally moved uneasily in his sleep and sighed heavily, but that was all.

"Maybe he ought to have a doctor, but what a doctor can do for him I don't know," thought Sam, and retired himself, sighing deeply. With Tom not himself the whole world seemed wrong.

Dick was on hand at the appointed time and Sam was glad to get up to meet him and know that Tom was still sleeping.

"Well, first of all, I'll have to tell you about Dad," said Dick, as he ran the auto up the road a bit, out of sight of Brill. "He is not nearly as well as I would like to see and the doctor says he must not dream of doing a stroke of work. So that leaves all that New York business, and that Western business, in my hands."

"Can you manage it, Dick?"

"I've got to manage it, Sam. And in the meantime I've got Mrs. Stanhope's affairs to look after, and also Dora's money matters. It is keeping me hustling, I can tell you. I never dreamed I would become such an out-and-out business fellow."

"It's fine of you to be able to do it, Dick. I am only sorry I can't help you. But some day Tom and I will finish up here and then we'll take hold."

"Sure, I know that. But now let us drop business. Tell me all about Tom. Just how has he been acting? I know you didn't want to let out in front of the girls."

"Well, Tom is a problem, Dick. Sometimes he acts as bright as ever and then he seems to be clean off." And then, in as few words as possible, Sam related the particulars of his brother's doings since he had returned to Brill. As he proceeded Dick's face grew very thoughtful.

"I don't like this at all," he said flatly. "Maybe after all it would be much better to send Tom home and place him under the care of a specialist. If he remains here there is no telling what he will do next. Supposing Spud or Stanley had been drowned in that well hole?" and Dick gave a shiver.

"Yes, but how are you going to get him home if he won't go?"

"Do you think he'll object?"

"Yes, Dick. But you can try him, if you wish," concluded Sam. And then the pair returned to the college grounds.

By this time Tom had come below and was looking for them.

"If you were going to take a ride why didn't you let me know?" he grumbled. "I'd like to run that car a bit before Dick goes back."

"Say, Tom, why not return to Cedarville with me and Dora?" asked Dick, kindly. "I am sure the trip would do you good, and when you got there you could take a good, long rest."

"Humph! all at me to rest, eh? Well, I'm not going to rest; I'm going to study and get through here just as soon as possible." Tom straightened up. "Now, don't you two think I can't do it, for I can. I feel stronger every day. That crack I got on the head was a fierce one, I admit, but it isn't going to knock me out, not by a long shot! In a few weeks I'll be as strong as ever."

Dick and Sam looked at each other in dismay. Clearly it was out of the question to try to argue with Tom, who had always been more or less headstrong.

"All right then, stay," said Dick. "But take it easy, Tom, and do what Sam tells you to." A little later Dick drew Sam to one side and asked him to keep a close watch on his brother.

"I'll do my best."

"And notify me at once if anything goes wrong," added Dick. Then he took the next quarter of an hour to visit with Songbird and some of his other old chums. Spud hailed him with delight and even Stanley smiled warmly as he shook hands.

"Stanley, I want to ask you to bear with poor Tom," said Dick, as he continued to hold the other's hand. "He isn't himself at all, and you ought to be able to see it. Sam and I want him to go home and consult a specialist, but he won't do it. I don't know what to make of him. What he did was terrible, and I am sure he wouldn't have done it if he was in his right mind."

"Maybe," returned Stanley, hesitatingly. "I've been talking it over with Spud and maybe I was a little harsh. But to be tumbled in that well hole, in the mud and water, made me mad clean through."

"It would make anybody mad, and I wouldn't stand for it either, if Tom was in his right mind. But you can see how it is. Sam and I feel terrible over it. I want you to forgive him, and

I want you and Spud and Songbird to help Sam watch him."

"Why, do you think he'll do something desperate?" asked Stanley, curiously.

"I don't know what to think. If a fellow is out of his head he is liable to do almost anything. I want him watched, and what is more, I'd like you fellows to keep this to yourselves. I don't want the whole college to know it."

"You can trust me to keep mum," said Spud, promptly.

"I shan't say a word," added Songbird. "I think too much of Tom. Why, he is one of the finest fellows in the world when he is all right!"

"All right, I'll keep quiet too," said Stanley. "And I won't hold anything against him. But you had better watch him pretty closely," was the warning.

Of course Tom wanted to know all about his father's business and Dick told him as much as he thought was necessary. He did not want to worry his sick brother and so kept back a good deal of what he had related to Sam.

"Don't you worry about me, Dick!" cried Tom, on parting. "I'll be all right!" And he waved his hand gaily, and so did Sam, as the big touring car moved away in the direction of Ashton.

Fortunately for the boys, the lessons that day

were not hard and Tom and Sam came through without missing. Then followed a settling down to the work of the term; and thus a week slipped by.

Day by day Sam watched Tom closely. He made his brother take his pills regularly and also made him take outdoor exercise, and aided him as much as possible in his studies and with his themes. All the others were very friendly, and even Stanley came up and told Tom that he was sorry he had been so harsh.

"Well, I don't blame you, Stanley," said Tom, frankly. "It was a mighty poor joke. I don't see how I did it." And there the matter was dropped.

It was ideal weather for outdoor sports and sometimes the lads would go out for a game of baseball, or football, just as the whim seized them. Of course the college had its regular teams on the diamond and the gridiron, but the Rovers did not care enough for the sport to try for these, even though they had made creditable records at Putnam Hall.

"Great news!" cried Tom, coming into the gymnasium one afternoon, after playing with some of the students on the campus.

"What's that?" asked several, curiously.

"A couple of moving picture men from Chicago have leased Cameron's Hall in Ashton and they are going to open a moving picture theater next week. Won't that be fine? I love the movies, and now we'll be able to go there whenever we want to."

CHAPTER VIII

THE JOKE ON WILLIAM PHILANDER

THE news Tom had brought created much interest in Brill. In the past anything in the shape of public amusement for the students had been scarce. Once in a while a cheap theatrical company would stop at Ashton and give a performance, but usually it was of such a poor order that if the boys went they would poke fun at it.

"How do you know it will be any good, Tom?" asked Songbird.

"Oh, I'm not sure that it will be. But the druggist told me that the men were well-known in the movies and had some first-class show-houses elsewhere, so I'm hoping it will be all right."

"Is it going to be a five or ten-cent house?" asked another.

"Five in the afternoon and ten at night."

"Then I'm going to begin to save my pennies," announced Spud, seriously. "I've got two saved already and if I am careful for the next month or two I'll have enough to buy a ticket."

"That is, provided I'll lend you one cent," added Tom, and this caused a general grin. He looked around and saw William Philander approaching. "Hi, Tubblets!" he called out. "Here's a job for you." And he waved his hand quickly for the dudish student to approach.

"Now, no more jokes, Tom Rover," was the warning of the stylishly-dressed one. "No more jokes."

"Jokes?" repeated Tom. "This is a job—a splendid situation—open to just such a handsome, well-proportioned young gentleman like yourself."

"What—ah—do you want?" asked William Philander, curiously.

"Wouldn't you like to assist during the evening at a new entertainment at Ashton? A couple of gentlemen are getting up an entertainment for the benefit of the ladies and gentlemen and they wish the aid of a real nice young man, to show the folks to their seats and make them comfortable, and all that. And maybe they'll want you to sing—just to help things along, you know."

"Oh, is that it?" and the dudish student's

face brightened. On several occasions he had assisted at charity bazaars and the like, and had been in his element among the well-dressed girls and their mothers.

"I think you would just fill the bill, Willie," went on Tom. "You are the best looking fellow here, and of course we know nobody dresses quite as well as you do."

"Oh, yes, of course—it's very kind to mention that, Tom," and William Philander commenced to swell up with pride. "Yes, I do try to keep up with the fashions. But about this entertainment. Who is getting it up and what benefit is it for?"

"Two gentlemen named Carr and Beckwith are getting it up. I don't know about the benefit. You can find out about that from them. But it's a splendid chance to show what you can do. You know all about showing folks to seats, and all that, don't you?"

"Why, yes, of course."

"And you could sing, eh?"

"Well,—ah—I might render that spring song—'Come Where the Flowers are Blooming, Dearest Mary.'"

"Just the cheese—I mean it would be fine, Tubby. They'd all go wild about that song. It's the same one you sang for the Prince of

Moneco, isn't it?—or was it the Duke of Twisters?"

"I—er—I never sang for those folks, Tom—I sang it at the Ladies Aid of the Golden Hope Society, and at the Quarterly Gathering of the Poladic Society."

"Yes, yes, I remember now. Well, you are just the one to fill the bill, Bill, yes, you are."

"Please don't call me Bill, it's horrid. But where shall I find out about this—er—entertainment?"

"At Carter's new drug-store. The gentlemen are to be there Saturday afternoon, to make all arrangements. You go by all means—I know they will be delighted to have your assistance."

"This isn't a—er—a joke, Tom?" asked William Philander, suspiciously.

"They want somebody, I tell you, honest. Don't they, Jepson?" went on Tom, turning to a lad who had been to Ashton with him.

"They sure do," answered Jepson, and then turned away to hide the broad grin on his face.

"How long is the entertainment to last?"

"You will have to get all the information from the gentlemen," answered Tom, calmly. "Just go down to the drug store and ask for Mr. Carr and Mr. Beckwith, and they'll tell you all about it. It's a fine chance for you, Tubby," concluded

Tom, and then walked away, followed by his chums.

"Tom, what is the game?" demanded Sam, when they were out of hearing.

"We'll go down to the drug store Saturday afternoon and see," was the reply.

"Are Carr and Beckwith the moving picture men?"

"Yes, and they want a young man to play usher, and do a lot of other things—one who can sing preferred," and the fun-loving Tom grinned broadly.

"Oh, Tom, and you would send William Philander there!" cried Songbird. "Such a dude as he is! He'll never forgive you!"

"There is seven dollars a week in it to start," answered the fun-loving Rover calmly, and this made all in the crowd roar, for they knew how rich Tubbs was and how working for seven dollars a week would appeal to him.

This conversation occurred on Thursday and the crowd of boys waited impatiently for Saturday to come. Sam was glad to notice that Tom seemed to improve daily and was acting very much like his old self.

On Saturday, directly after lunch, Sam and Tom saw William Philander start off for Ashton. He was stylishly dressed as usual and carried a gold-headed cane, and in his buttonhole was a large carnation.

"Now for the fun!" cried Tom, and he and Sam quickly gathered their chums together and all went after the dude, but kept out of his sight.

The drug store that Wlliam Philander was bound for was located on a corner, with doors opening on both streets. On the side street there was also an ordinary window, and both doors and window were wide open.

"We'll go around to the side and watch him," suggested Tom, and this was done.

Sprucing up, so as to look his very best, William Philander strode into the drug store. As it chanced, several young ladies of the town were having soda at the fountain, and as he had once met one of them, he made a most profound bow, lifting his hat as he did so. Then he approached the proprietor of the shop, who was putting up a prescription at the rear counter, close to the open window.

"Mr. Carter I believe?" he lisped.

"Yes, sir. What can I do for you?"

"I am Mr. William Philander Tubbs, from Brill College," was the lofty answer. "Perhaps you have heard of me. I came in to meet two gentlemen, Mr. Carr and Mr. Beckwith. Are they here?"

"Not yet, Mr—er—Mr. Phillips?"

"No, no, Mr. William Philander Tubbs. When will they be here, may I ask?"

"I expect 'em any moment, Mr—er—Mr. Tubbs."

"Then I'll wait for them," answered the dude, and sank down in a chair.

"Have you got an interest in that show?" asked the druggist, as he continued to compound the prescription.

"Not yet, but I may have," answered William Philander, calmly. "It will be quite a grand affair, I presume."

"They say it will be the best Ashton ever had."

"Is that so! Then I am very glad I came to take part," went on William Philander, warming up. "I am sure I can be of great service to Messrs. Carr and Beckwith. I have had a great deal of experience, you know."

"Thought you said you were from Brill?"

"Oh, yes, but, don't you know, I have assisted at many entertainments," gushed William Philander. "Why, some entertainments would have been absolute failures if I had not taken part."

"Hum, is that so!" returned the druggist. Tubbs' dudish ways did not strike him very favorably. "Well, here is Mr. Beckwith now, you can tell him about it," he added.

A burly, red-faced man, with a heavy moustache, had entered. He was evidently in a hurry and full of business.

"Anybody call about that job, Mr. Carter?" he asked, abruptly.

"This young man wants to see you," answered the druggist, and indicated William Philander.

"You are Mr. Beckwith?"

"Yes."

"Permit me," and the stylish-dressed student presented his card. "I was told you were getting up an entertainment and needed some assistance," continued William Philander. "Now I have had a great deal of experience in that line, and the ladies always seem to be glad to see me. I can aid in getting up the proper programme, and all that, you know. I was on the committee of the Charity Bazaar, and the Plainville Dog Show, and the Ladies' Aid of the Golden Hope Society, and the Blue Banner Social, and——"

"Say, what are you pouring into me?" gasped Mr. Beckwith, in astonishment. "Do you think I am running a pink tea, or a ladies' sewing circle? I don't need anybody to help me to get up a programme; my partner, Mr. Carr, attends to that end of it. What I need is a strong, willing fellow to take tickets and usher folks to seats, and keep the floor free of rubbish, and all that."

"W-h-a-t!" shrieked William Philander. "You—you—what sort of an entertainment are you going to give?" he faltered.

"Why, didn't you know? We are going to open the Eclipse Moving Picture Theater, in Cameron's Hall, over yonder. We advertised for a young man, to take tickets, usher, and make himself generally useful. We'll have a little vaudeville with the photo plays, and if the young fellow can sing, or dance, we'll give him a chance at it."

"Oh, dear me! Did you ever!" gasped poor William Philander. And then, as he saw that the girls at the soda fountain had heard all that was going on, he turned red.

"I hardly think you will do for the job," went on the moving picture man. "You don't look—er—well, strong enough."

"Job," wailed William Philander. "I—er—I don't want any job! Oh, this is dreadful, horrible! It's one of Tom Rover's jokes! I might have known it. Sent me all the way to Ashton to try to get a position in a horrid moving picture show! Oh, this is the worst ever!" And looking the picture of despair, poor Tubbs rushed from the drug store, with the laughter of the proprietor, the show man, and the girls ringing in his ears.

From the window and the side door Tom, Sam, and the others had seen and heard all that took place. They had all they could do to suppress their mirth, and when Tubbs came storming out of the drug store they lost no time in disappearing out of sight behind the building. They watched the stylishly-dressed student prance down the street, brandishing his cane viciously in the air.

"Just wait till he catches you, Tom," remarked Spud.

"He'll about half kill you," added Stanley.

"Oh, I guess I can stand it," answered the fun-loving Rover, calmly.

"It was rather a rough joke," was Sam's comment.

"Oh, he needs something like that, to take the awful conceit out of him," came from Songbird. "Why, he is getting worse and worse every day. Half the students are down on him. This may do him good."

"I doubt if you can make William Philander improve," was Stanley's comment. "The only thing that will do it is to send him off to sea, or on a ranch, and make him rough it for a while."

Tom expected to see Tubbs that evening, but the dudish student kept out of sight. He did not show himself until Sunday afternoon, and then he had but little to say. But he eyed Tom in a manner that was new to William Philander.

"He is going to get back at you, Tom," said Sam. "Better keep your eyes open."

On Monday afternoon Tom and Sam went down to the water for a short row. They came back just before supper and rushed up to their room to fix up a bit.

"Hello, the door is locked!" cried Tom, trying it.

"And the keyhole is plugged," added Sam, taking a look.

Then the brothers looked at each other.

"I guess William Philander Tubbs did it," said Tom.

CHAPTER IX

WILLIAM PHILANDER TURNS THE TABLES

It was useless to try to open the door. The lock was filled up with a wad of paper that refused to budge.

"If it's only paper we can burn it out," suggested Sam. "But it may scorch the door."

"We'll go through by the way of Songbird's room," said Tom.

There was a door connecting the two rooms. It was not supposed to be used, for one of the beds was against it. But the bed was rolled to one side by Tom. Songbird and his roommate had already gone below.

"Here's the key," said Sam, bringing it from a nearby nail. "It's a wonder William Philander didn't plug this keyhole, too."

"Maybe he didn't have time," answered Tom. "Always supposing it really was Tubbs."

"That's so—it may have been somebody else."

The connecting door was unlocked and Tom

and Sam walked into their own apartment. Both gave a cry of astonishment.

And not without reason. The room had been "stacked," and every boy who has ever attended boarding school or college knows what that means. In the center of the room lay the parts of the two beds in a heap and on top of those parts were piled a miscellaneous collection of books, chairs, clothing, the table and bureau, looking glass, an empty water pitcher, football, baseball bats, shoes, bed clothing, rugs, papers, pens, pencils, soap, caps, a steamer trunk from the closet, several framed photographs, some college banners, and a score of other articles. On the very top of the heap was a fancy sofa pillow Nellie had given to Tom and to this was pinned a card, on which was written, in a disguised scrawl:

Hoping you will enjoy your job!

"It was William Philander all right enough," murmured Sam, as he and his brother inspected the card. "You sent him to one job, and he is sending us to another," and he heaved a deep sigh.

"Some work, Sammy," returned Tom. "Well, we can't go at it now—it will take us two hours to straighten things up. We'll do it after supper."

"Going after Tubbs for this?"

"What's the use? I don't blame him for getting back at us. I guess, after all, that joke I played on him was rather rough," replied Tom.

It took the best part of three hours to put the room back into shape. Some ink had been spilled on one of the mattresses, and the glass over one of the photographs had been broken, but that was all the real damage that had been done, and it looked to be accidental. The wad of paper in the keyhole was picked out piecemeal by means of a big fishhook. The key was in the heap on the floor, having been flung through the open transom after the door was locked and plugged.

"Well, he got back at you right enough," said Songbird, while the room was being re-arranged.

"Dot's chust vot he did, py golly!" came from Max Spangler.

After this incident the boys settled down to their studies for the best part of a week. Tom was now doing very well, although he still complained of his head.

"I've got an idea," said Sam, one afternoon, after the Eclipse photo playhouse in Ashton had been opened. "Why can't we make up a party some afternoon or evening and take the girls to the show?"

"I thought of that," answered Tom. "But don't you think it would be best for us to go alone first and see what sort of a place it is? Some of these country show places have pretty rough audiences."

"Oh, Ashton isn't such a common town as that, Tom. But maybe it would be better to size it up first. What do you say if we go down next Wednesday evening? We might make up a little party, with Songbird and the others."

"That suits me."

The matter was talked over with the others, and it was speedily arranged that nine of the students should go, including Sam, Tom, Songbird, and Spud. Stanley could not get away, and Max had some lessons he wanted to make up.

"I hope they have some thrilling films," said Tom, when the time came to leave for Ashton. "I hate these wishy-washy love stories and would-be funny scenes. I once saw a shipwreck that was fine, and a slide down a mountainside that couldn't be beaten."

"Well, we'll have to take what comes," said Sam. "I understand they change the pictures twice a week."

When the students arrived at the playhouse in Ashton an agreeable surprise awaited them. Instead of the dingy hall they had expected to see, they saw that the place had been completely transformed. There was a large electric sign over the door, and several big billboards announced the various attractions. A crowd was purchasing tickets at the booth in front, and already the showhouse was half filled for the first performance of the evening.

"'Her First Love,'" read Tom, from a billboard. "That sounds a little mushy. 'Broncho Bill's Reward,'" he went on. "That might be interesting. 'Lost in the Ice Fields of Alaska, in Two Parts.' Say, that sounds as if it might be something worth while," he added, brightening up.

"Yes, I'd like to see some pictures of Alaska," returned Songbird.

"Provided they weren't taken in Hoboken, or somewhere like that," answered Sam. "Some of these moving pictures are great fakes. They take real scenes in China right in New York City, and show you the bottom of the sea, taken on the sixth floor of an office building in Chicago!"

"Never mind, I guess we'll get our money's worth," said another of the students, and then the crowd passed inside, each youth buying his own ticket, as was the usual custom.

They managed to get seats almost in the center of the hall, which was long and narrow, just the shape for such an exhibition. They noticed that a tall, lanky town boy was usher, and Tom nudged Sam in the ribs.

"Just think, William Philander might have had that job!" he chuckled.

"Well, you did the best you could for him," answered Sam, dryly.

The end of a funny reel was being shown and the audience was laughing heartily. Then came an illustrated song, sung by a young woman with a fairly good voice, and after that "Broncho Bill's Reward," a short drama of the plains, with cowboys and cattle thieves, and a sheriff, who aided Broncho Bill to get back his employer's cattle and win the hand of the girl he loved.

"Maybe you could write some verses about that girl," suggested Sam to Songbird, in a whisper. "You could call it 'The Cowboy's Sweetheart,' or something like that."

"So I could," murmured the would-be poet, and immediately commenced to make up rhymes, which he scribbled on some paper in the dark.

At last came the well-advertised drama, "Lost

Thus the talk ran on, all of the students being enthusiastic over the production. The only one who was rather quiet was Tom, and soon Sam noticed this.

"What's the matter, Tom; don't you feel well?" he asked, anxiously.

"Nothing extra," was the answer, and Tom put his hands to his eyes. "I guess that moving picture strained my head too much. But it was great—best picture I ever saw! Say, I'd like to go to Alaska once, wouldn't you, Sam?"

"Yes, but not to be caught in the ice and snow like that," returned the younger Rover boy. "Say, it's a good show for the girls, all right," he went on.

"Fine. We'll take 'em as soon as we can arrange it."

All the way back to Brill the students talked about the wonderful Alaskan film, which had really been taken on the spot and had cost a good deal of money. Evidently in opening the new photo playhouse Messrs. Carr and Beckwith had resolved to give the audiences their money's worth.

It was a good advertisement, too, for not only did the town people flock to the place, but the college students told their friends, and the next evening a score or more of the boys attended the performance. The dimes flowed in steadily, much to the delight of the owners of the project.

That evening Sam noticed that Tom was quite feverish and he advised his brother to take an extra pill, to quiet him.

"Oh, all I need is sleep," said Tom. "That picture hurt my eyes a little. After they are rested I'll be all right." And then he undressed and retired.

Sam had been asleep about two hours when he awoke with a start. He sat up, and in the dim light of the room saw his brother thrashing wildly in the bed.

"Give me the nuggets!" murmured poor Tom, in a nightmare. "I must have the money! Ha, the biggest nugget in Alaska!" He clutched at the pillow. "Out of my way, I say! It is mine! Look, it is snowing! Where is the trail? We are lost! See the ice and snow! Lost! lost! lost!" And Tom floundered around more wildly than ever.

Sam leaped out of bed, and, catching his brother by the arm, shook him vigorously.

"Tom! Tom! wake up!" he cried. "You're asleep! Wake up! You are not in Alaska! Wake up!"

"Oh, the ice and snow! And the trail is lost! We shall die! Can nothing save——

Er—er—eh? What's the—the matter?" stammered Tom, and suddenly opened his eyes. "What are you shaking me for, Sam?" he demanded.

"You've got a nightmare, Tom, and you were shouting to beat the band!"

"Was I? Say, I—I thought I was in Alaska, right in that field of snow and ice. And I was lost! Gosh! what a scare I had!" And poor Tom fairly trembled.

"Well, go to sleep and try to forget it," said Sam, and Tom laid down again, and soon dropped off. Sam also retired once more, but he was much troubled.

"I guess it didn't do Tom any good to go to that show," he reasoned.

CHAPTER X

IN WHICH TOM DISAPPEARS

SAM was the first one up in the morning. He found Tom thrashing around in his bed. He had an uncertain look in his eyes and was feverish.

"How do you feel, Tom?" he asked, sitting down and taking his brother's hand.

"Not as good as usual," was the reply. Tom put his hand to his head, as of old. "I've got a fierce pain here," he added.

"Shall I send for a doctor?"

"No, I'll keep quiet and maybe it will go over, Sam."

"All right, I'll have you excused from lessons."

Sam dressed and went below, and after breakfast came up again. He found Tom sound asleep.

"I guess sleep will do him as much good as anything," he told himself, and went out again, closing the door softly.

Sam had two classes to attend before dinner, so it was not until quarter to twelve that he had a chance to run up to the room again. To his surprise Tom was gone.

"Songbird, did you see Tom?" he called to his chum, who was in the next room.

"No."

"He's gone, and I left him sound asleep when I went to lessons."

"Oh, he must be somewhere around," suggested the would-be poet of the college. "Maybe he's taking a bath."

"I'll find out," said Sam.

On the way to the bathroom he met Spud and asked about Tom.

"Why, I saw Tom about eleven o'clock," said Spud. "He told me he was going to town to see a doctor."

"Doctor Havens?"

"Yes."

"Oh, all right," and Sam felt much relieved. He went to dinner with the others and then waited for Tom's return. A full hour went by and still Tom did not show himself, and then Sam sought out Spud once more.

"How did Tom act when he went away, Spud?"

"Act? What do you mean?"

"Was he all right?"

"Well, to tell the truth, Sam, I think he looked a bit strange in his eyes. But I guess he was all right. I'd not worry too much if I was you. He'll be back before long. Maybe Doctor Havens was out and he had to wait."

"That's so."

Presently Sam had a lecture to attend and went off to it. At half-past three he was free once more and hurried again to his room. Tom was still absent, and nobody seemed to know anything about him.

"I guess I had better go to town and see where he is," thought Sam, and he asked Songbird if he wanted to go along.

"Yes, I'll go, Sam. But don't worry so much—I'm certain Tom is O. K."

"Maybe, Songbird. But you know how queer he acted. He didn't seem to be able to get over that crack in his head."

"Well, it was an awful blow, Sam. It would have killed some people."

Before long the pair were on their way to Ashton. About half way to the town they met two students who had been away from Brill for several days.

"Did you come from Ashton, Cabot?" asked Sam, of one of the boys.

"We did.'"

"See anything of my brother Tom?"

"No."

"I think I saw him," said the other student, a fellow named Lambert.

"Where?"

"Down at the depot. I was looking for my baggage. I think I saw him near the freight house."

"Was he alone?"

"Yes, so far as I know. Why, what's wrong, Rover?"

"Oh, nothing, only I want to find him," said Sam, and to avoid further questioning, he hurried on, pulling Songbird with him.

"If Tom was at the freight house he must have been taking a walk," suggested Songbird.

"Perhaps; but I am awfully worried about this."

It did not take the two students long to reach Ashton, and Sam went directly to the home of Doctor Havens, located in a grove of trees on a side street. A man was washing down the front piazza with a pail of water.

"Is the doctor in?" asked Sam.

"No, sir, he won't he in until about six o'clock," said the man.

"How long has he been gone, may I ask?"

"He went to the city directly after breakfast this morning, for a consultation with some other doctors."

"He hasn't any assistant?"

"No, sir, but he said if anybody needed a doctor in a hurry to call old Doctor Slate."

"Where does he live?"

"In the big white house on the hill, opposite the depot."

"I know the place," put in Songbird.

"We'll go there," said Sam. "Much obliged," he added, to the man.

"Maybe Tom went there and that is how Lambert came to see him near the freight house," suggested Songbird.

"We'll soon know," returned the youngest Rover.

It did not take the students long to cross the railroad tracks and reach Doctor Slate's residence. They found the old doctor out in his garden, tying up some bushes. He was a white-haired gentleman and had given up his regular practice some years before.

"No, there has been no young man to see me," he said, in answer to Sam's question. "Old Mrs. Powers was in, and Pop Slocum, the negro, and that's all."

"In that case, Tom must be hanging around

town, waiting for Doctor Havens to return," said Songbird.

"It's a puzzle to me," said Sam, with a deep sigh, and he and his chum walked slowly away.

"I wouldn't worry so much, Sam," said Songbird, sympathetically. "I am sure it will be all right."

"It would be if Tom was all right in his head, Songbird. But you know how he acted that day Stanley and Spud went into the old well hole, and——"

"Well, what could happen to him in Ashton, such a sleepy country town as this is? Oh, he's around somewhere and will soon turn up, take my word for it."

They found the depot deserted, for it was a time of day when there were no trains. Then they walked up the main street, past the stores and the Eclipse photo playhouse. The afternoon performance was just over at the show place and a crowd of about a hundred, mostly women and children, was pouring forth. In the crowd were a burly, jolly looking farmer and a pretty girl, his daughter.

"Why, Mr. Sanderson!" cried Songbird, his face lighting up. "And you, Minnie! This is a surprise!" and he shook hands.

"Oh!" cried the girl, and smiled sweetly. "I didn't expect to see you here."

"We were doing some tradin' in town and thought we'd run in and see the movin' picters," said Mr. Sanderson, who knew the boys well. "They sure are great."

"We came in to find Tom," said Sam, as he, too, shook hands. He and his brothers had once done Minnie Sanderson a great service, the particulars of which I have related in "The Rover Boys at College." Since that time Songbird had frequently visited the Sanderson homestead, to call on Minnie, whom he regarded as the nicest young lady of his acquaintance.

"To find Tom?" repeated Minnie.

"Yes. Have you seen him?"

"I saw him about noon time," said Mr. Sanderson.

"Where?"

"Why, he was walking along the road to Hope Seminary."

"The road to Hope?" cried Sam. "Are you sure?"

"Tolerably sure, Sam. I was drivin' rather fast an' didn't take much of a look. But I reckon it was Tom."

"Maybe he went there to call on Nellie," suggested Songbird.

"This mixes me up," murmured Sam. "I don't know what to think."

"I trust there is nothing wrong, Sam," said Minnie, sweetly. She counted the Rovers among her warmest friends.

"I—I hope not, and yet I am very much worried. You see, Tom hasn't been just himself ever since he got that blow on the head. He came to Ashton to see a doctor, but the doctor was away on business. Now I can't find him anywhere."

"If you want to go to Hope I'll drive you there," said Mr. Sanderson. "I've got to go there anyway—to see about some potatoes they wanted. Minnie said she would stay in town and do some more shopping, until I got back. But I've only got a buggy big enough for two," added the farmer.

"I could stay in town with Minnie until you got back," said Songbird, eagerly, to Sam. "I could keep my eyes open for Tom."

"We could both look for him," added the girl. It pleased her to think she might have the would-be poet's company.

The matter was talked over for several minutes and then it was agreed that Sam should ride over to the seminary with the farmer.

"You won't have to hurry back," said Songbird, on parting. "If it gets too late Minnie and I can go over to the hotel for supper," and he smiled at the girl, who blushed and smiled in return.

Mr. Sanderson had always owned some excellent horses and the mare attached to his buggy was a swift animal. He and Sam got into the turnout, and away they went with a whirl, soon leaving Ashton behind.

"This year the seminary is going to buy all its potatoes from me," explained the farmer. "And they get their cabbages, and carrots and turnips from me, too, and a good many of their eggs and chickens. They are quite a customer, and I want to do my best to please 'em."

"It's a fine place," returned Sam. "Just as good as Brill."

"So it is, Sam. By the way, how is Dick makin' out? I understand he was lookin' after your father's business."

"He is, and he is getting along very well. Of course, our lawyer is helping him, for some matters are in an awful tangle."

"That feller who hit Tom over the head ought to have been put in jail."

"Well, he is going to lose most of his property—or at least, he had to give up what belonged to Dad. The lawyer thinks that will be punishment enough. We thought of prosecuting the bunch, but Dad is in such bad health he didn't want to bother. Besides, one of the crowd, Josiah Crabtree, broke his leg in two places and he will be a cripple for life."

"Serves the rascal right! He had no business to interfere with you, and with that Mrs. Stanhope an' her daughter. I ain't got no sympathy to waste on sech cattle," snorted the straight-minded farmer.

Presently they came in sight of Hope Seminary and Mr. Sanderson drove around to a side door, to interview the housekeeper. Sam walked around to the front, and rang the doorbell, and a maid answered his summons.

"I would like to see Miss Grace Laning," he said. "Or, if she isn't in, her sister, Miss Nellie."

"Yes, sir," and the girl ushered the young collegian into the reception room.

A few minutes later Grace appeared. She looked at Sam in surprise.

"Why, I thought you wrote you'd come next Tuesday," she cried.

"So I did, Grace. But this time I've come about Tom. Have you seen him?"

"Tom? No. Did he come here?"

"I thought he might have come. Mr. Sanderson saw him on the road, headed in this direction."

"Oh, Sam, you look so—so alarmed! What is it? What do you think has happened?"

"I don't know what has happened, Grace. But something is wrong, I feel sure of it," answered Sam, with conviction. "Tom is missing, and I can't imagine what has become of him."

CHAPTER XI

WHAT THE GIRLS KNEW

After that, Sam related the particulars of what had occurred, to which Grace listened closely. As she did this, tears streamed down the cheeks of the girl.

"This will break Nellie's heart—if it isn't broken already," she faltered. "You know I wrote that I had something to tell you, Sam. It was about Nellie. But I can't tell you here—let us take a walk."

"All right. But I can't stay long—I must go back with Mr. Sanderson and continue this hunt for Tom."

"To be sure—I won't keep you but a few minutes." Grace led the way outside and down one of the campus walks. "You remember that time we came back from the auto ride?" she said.

"Of course."

"Well, when Nellie and I got to our room she

threw herself on the bed and cried as if her heart was breaking. I couldn't do anything with her. I wanted to find out what it was all about, but at first she wouldn't tell me a word. Then she said it was Tom—that he had acted so queerly when they took a walk in the park he had scared her."

"What did he do?"

"Oh, he talked so queer! He told Nellie he wished he had the *Dartaway* back, so that they could go on a honeymoon trip to the moon. And then he laughed and asked her if she would go on a camelback ride with him through the Sahara desert. And then he said he didn't want to get married until he could lay a big nugget of gold at her feet—and a lot of nonsense like that. She was awfully scared at first, but after a while he got more rational and then she felt a little better. But she couldn't get it off her mind, and it made her feel dreadful! And then, the other day, Tom sent her the queerest letter, full of all sorts of the wildest kind of nonsense—about going to the North Pole and bringing the pole back with him, and about sending her a pair of slippers, to wear in place of gloves, and asking her to send him a red and blue handkerchief, to keep his head from aching. And he wrote that he didn't think he was cut out for college, that he would rather shovel nuggets in a gold mine—that is just what he wrote—'shovel nuggets in a gold mine!' Oh, such a mixed-up letter you never read! And it made Nellie cry again. Oh, Sam, what does it mean?"

He shook his head and gave a deep sigh.

"I don't know, Grace. It scares me almost as much as it has Nellie. Maybe Tom ought to be put in a sanitarium."

"Oh, do you think he is really out of his mind?"

"It almost looks that way. Poor Tom! and he was always so bright and full of fun!"

"But what can—Oh, Sam, here is Nellie now!" cried Grace, as her sister appeared and ran towards them.

"Oh, Sam, I just met Mr. Sanderson and he said you were looking for Tom!" cried Nellie, as she came closer.

"That's true, Nellie."

"He hasn't been here—at least I haven't seen him."

"So Grace just told me," Sam tried to look at the girl in front of him, but had to turn his gaze away. He knew only too well how much Nellie thought of his brother.

"Did he—he run away?" burst out Nellie.

"I don't know about that, Nellie," said Sam,

and told his story over again, just as he had related it to her sister.

Nellie burst into tears, and Sam and Grace did their best to comfort her. Grace's own eyes were moist, and Sam had all he could do to keep from breaking down likewise.

"Oh, he is gone, I am sure of it!" cried Nellie. "He is not himself at all! For all we know he may have thrown himself into the river! Oh, what shall we do? What can we do?" and she wrung her hands.

"Don't take it so hard, Nellie, it may not be so bad after all," said her sister, soothingly. "Tom may be back to Brill by this time."

For several minutes the matter was talked over. Then Mr. Sanderson appeared, ready to return to Ashton for his daughter.

"I'll help you hunt for Tom," said the bluff farmer. "I know he must be somewhere around. Don't you worry so," for he could see that Nellie had been crying.

"Send word at once, when you do find him," begged Nellie, as the buggy drove away, and Sam promised.

On the way back to town but little was said. Near Brill they met quite a few students and the youngest Rover asked them if they had seen his brother. All replied in the negative.

When Ashton was reached it was dark, and they drove around to the hotel. Songbird and Minnie had been dining, and the student asked Mr. Sanderson and Sam to have something.

"No, I don't care to eat just now," said Sam. "I'll take another look around," and he left the Sandersons and Songbird together.

But Sam's walk around the town was productive of no results. He called again on the two doctors, only to be told that Tom had not shown himself at either place. At the depot nobody seemed to remember seeing him. The youth visited several stores where Tom was known, but none of the clerks had seen the missing one.

"I suppose all I can do is to return to Brill and wait," said Sam, on rejoining those at the hotel. "I might send out a general alarm, but I'd hate to do that and then have Tom walk in as if nothing unusual had happened."

"And it would be just like him to do it," returned Songbird.

It was nearly ten o'clock when Sam and his chum returned to the college. Tom had not yet shown himself, nor had he sent in any word. His books and his clothing were exactly as he had left them.

"Well, he didn't take anything with him," was Sam's comment, as several of his chums came in to sympathize with him. "That looks as if he hadn't meant to go far."

"Oh, he'll be back, don't worry," said Spud, optimistically.

All did their best to cheer poor Sam up, but this did little good. Sam was much worried and his face showed it.

"I don't know what to do," he said. "I certainly don't feel like going to bed."

One of the proctors had heard that Tom was missing and came to the room to see about it. Sam told him all he knew and the proctor said he would immediately report the case to Doctor Wallington.

"You know he can't stay out as late as this without permission," observed the proctor.

"Permission or no permission I wish he was here," answered Sam. "He is sick and I am very much worried about him." And then the proctor left.

An hour dragged by and the other students went to bed. Sam sat up in an easy chair, trying to doze, but starting up at every sound. He tried to figure out what would be best for him to do, but could reach no satisfactory conclusion. He looked out of the window. The moon was setting and soon all became dark. A wagon rattled by on the roadway beyond the campus, and the clock in the college tower tolled out the hour of midnight.

"This is simply awful!" murmured Sam, as he walked back to the easy chair and dropped down. "I wonder if I hadn't better send a message to Dick? But I can't do it until seven o'clock—the telegraph office is closed."

At last Sam became so worn out that he could keep his eyes open no longer. He flung himself on his bed, dressed as he was, and fell into a fitful doze. And thus the hours went by until the sun shone over the hills in the East.

"Did he come in?" It was a question put by Songbird, as he came to the door.

"No."

"Say, Sam, this is strange. What are you going to do?"

"I don't know—telegraph to Dick and send out a general alarm, I guess."

"You don't think he simply ran away, do you?"

"What, without telling me? You know better than that, Songbird."

"Then he must have wandered off while he was out of his mind. Maybe he's somewhere in the woods around here."

"Maybe. I only hope he isn't hurt."

"Well, if I can do anything, let me know,"

answered Songbird, and stepped back into his room to dress.

As soon as possible Sam went to Doctor Wallington and talked the matter over with the head of Brill. The worthy doctor knew about the case already and was all sympathy.

"We had better send out a general alarm," he said. "And you can notify your folks. It was a mistake to let your brother come back here so soon after being hurt. You can take one of the carriages and drive down to Ashton at once, if you wish, and also drive around to some of the other places in this vicinity. Somebody must have seen your brother after he left here, or after Mr. Sanderson saw him."

"Would you mind if I take John Powell with me?" asked Sam. "I may need somebody to help me."

"Very well, Rover, he can go if he wishes."

"To be sure I'll go," said Songbird, when told of this. "And we'll find Tom, see if we don't," he added, by way of cheering Sam.

Sam waited until nine o'clock to see if Tom would show himself and then he and Songbird drove over the Ashton. A search lasting the best part of an hour followed, but nothing new was learned. Then, rather reluctantly—for he knew that Dick was having trouble enough attending to their father's affairs—he sent a telegram to his big brother, telling of Tom's disappearance, and adding that he would telegraph again, if anything new turned up.

In driving over to Hope Seminary Mr. Sanderson had pointed out to Sam the spot where he had seen—or thought he had seen—Tom. Sam now determined to visit that spot and see if from that point he could not get on the trail of his brother.

The place was near a turn of the road and just beyond was another road. At the forks stood an old stone house, wherein lived an old basket-maker named Rater. The girls of Hope often bought baskets from the man just to help him along.

Sam and Songbird found Rater sitting on a side porch of his home, with his basket-making materials scattered around him. He was a tall, thin man, somewhat deaf, but with a pair of sharp eyes.

"Come to buy a basket?" he asked, briskly.

"No, I came for a little information, if you can give it, Mr. Rater," replied Sam.

"What do you want to know?"

"Were you here yesterday?"

"I sure was—all day long."

"Did you see anything of my brother?" went

on Sam. "He is a little larger than I am, and here is his picture," and the youngest Rover produced a photograph he had brought along.

The old basketmaker looked at the photograph carefully.

"Why, yes, I see that feller," he said slowly. "He stopped at my gate fer a minute or two. He acted sort o' strange."

"In what way?"

"He didn't speak to me, he spoke to hisself. Said something about a basketful o' nuggets. I asked him if he wanted to buy a basket, but he only shook his head an' said somethin' about wantin' to git the nuggets o' gold first. Then, all of a sudden like, he ran away."

"And which way did he go?" asked Sam, with interest.

"Up the Hoopville road," and the old basketmaker pointed to the side road which ran past his home.

"Did he have any baggage with him?" questioned Songbird.

"Nary a thing."

"Thank you for the information," said Sam, and passed over a quarter, which Rater pocketed with a broad smile. Ready money was scarce with him.

"We'll drive to Hoopville," said Sam, a minute later, as he and Songbird got in the buggy. "And we'll ask about Tom on the way."

A quarter of a mile was passed and they came to a lonely spot on the highway. Here, the only building in sight was a half tumbled down cottage belonging to a man named Hiram Duff. Duff pretended to be poor, but common report had it that he was a miser and fairly well to do.

"Going to stop here?" questioned Songbird, as they drove near.

"We might as well," returned Sam. "Old Duff is a tough customer, but in this case——"

He did not finish for at that instant a muffled cry came from the old cottage, startling both boys.

CHAPTER XII

AT HIRAM DUFF'S COTTAGE

"WHAT can that be?"

"Must be somebody in trouble!"

"Maybe it is old Duff!"

"Let us go and see!"

With these hasty exclamations both boys leaped from the carriage they occupied and ran towards the delapidated cottage. The cries continued, coming from somewhere in the interior.

"Wait—we'll look in the window first," suggested Sam. "Maybe old Duff is having a quarrel with one of his neighbors, and if so it might not be wise to interfere."

There was a window with small panes of glass close at hand, and going to this the two youths peered into the cottage. To their surprise they could see nobody. Both lower rooms of the old building seemed to be unoccupied.

"Let's go around to the rear. Maybe the sounds come from there," suggested Songbird.

There was a path full of weeds leading to a

rear porch that was almost ready to fall down. The back door stood partly open. Nobody was in sight.

"The call comes from somewhere inside," said Sam. "Come on in. But be on your guard, Songbird. We don't want to get into trouble."

Both lads crossed the rickety porch and entered what was the kitchen of the cottage. A musty odor prevaded the building, for old Duff usually kept everything tightly closed.

The place was in disorder, a chair being overturned and several cooking utensils littering the floor. On the stove, which was cold, lay a big carving knife.

"What do you want? Where are you?" called out Sam.

"Oh, help me! Get me out of here!" came the somewhat faint reply. "I am in the cellar!"

"In the cellar!" repeated Songbird. "Are you Mr. Duff?"

"Yes. Help me out, please."

Both boys looked around for a stairs, but there was none. Then, to one side of the kitchen floor, they saw a trap door. It was shut down and bolted by means of a plug stuck through two staples.

It was an easy matter to kick the plug away and raise the trap door. The boys peered down into the opening below and saw Hiram Duff sitting on the lower step of the stairs. He looked hollow-eyed and almost exhausted.

"What's the matter, Mr. Duff? How did you get shut up this way?" asked Sam, kindly.

"Oh, my! Oh, my!" sighed the old miser. "Ca—can't you help me up the stairs? I am so —so weak I can't hardly walk. Where is the rascal who shut me up this way? I'll have the police on him!"

"Did somebody shut you up in this cellar?" asked Sam, as he and Songbird crawled below to give the old man assistance. They saw that the cellar was merely a big hole in the ground and the stairs were very steep and not particularly safe.

"Yes, somebody got me to come down here and then locked that trap door on me," grumbled the miser. He got up with difficulty and crawled slowly to the kitchen, the boys coming after him to see that he did not fall back. "Oh, dear, what a time I have had of it!" he whined.

"When was this?" asked Songbird.

"I don't know—that is, I can't tell how long it was until I know what time it is now."

"It is half-past ten," answered Sam, consulting his watch.

"What! Do you mean half-past ten in the

morning?" burst out Hiram Duff. "If that's true then I've been down cellar all night—ever since yesterday afternoon! No wonder I was hungry and thirsty. I've got to have something to eat and drink soon, or I'll starve to death!" And he walked to the kitchen cupboard and got out some bread and meat. There was water in a pail on the bench and he took a long drink of this.

"Who was it locked you in the cellar?" asked Sam.

"Who be you boys?" asked the miser in return.

"We belong to Brill College. We were driving past and we heard you yell," answered Songbird.

"Yes, I thought I heard a carriage on the road, so I called as loud as I could. I did that ever since that fellow went away, but I guess nobody heard me—leastwise, they didn't pay no attention."

"Will you tell us how it all happened?" asked Sam, and then he added aside to Songbird. "Don't say anything about Tom." And the would-be poet of Brill nodded to show he understood.

"It was this way," answered Hiram Duff, dropping down on the chair Sam fixed for him.

"I was sitting on the back porch mending my coat when all of a sudden a fellow came around the corner of the house. He was a strange looking young fellow and he wore a funny looking cap pulled away down over his eyes. He asked me if I wasn't Hackler. I said I wasn't, that my name was Hiram Duff. Then he says, 'I knew it, I knew it! At last!' and sits down on the porch. I says, 'At last, what?' and he says something about a nugget of gold. He acted awful mysterious like, and finally he asks me if I'd like to own half of a big nugget of gold. I told him I certainly would."

"And then?" asked Sam, as the old miser paused to take a bite of bread and meat.

"Then he told a queer story about a nugget of gold brought down to this place from Alaska. He was very mysterious, and at last he said the nugget was right down in my cellar, and if I'd dig it up fer him he'd give me half. At first I thought he was fooling, or wasn't just right in his mind, but a nugget of gold—even a little one—isn't to be sneezed at, and it wouldn't cost me nuthing to go down cellar and look. So I starts to go down the stairs when he says to be careful, that he would look around, to make sure nobuddy was a-spying on him. He said the nugget was in the northwest corner. I went down, and the next thing I knew I heard a strange cry upstairs. 'You shan't rob me! The nugget is mine!' yells that fellow and bang! goes that trap door, and then he up and bolts it fast, so I couldn't open it. I calls to let me out, and he calls back for me to keep quiet until he got some friends, so I couldn't rob him of that nugget. Then he slammed around upstairs here something awful. At last he went away; and that's the last I seen or heard of him."

"What did you do? Didn't you try to get out?" questioned Songbird.

"For a long time I waited, thinking he would come back. And as he seemed so sure about the nugget I took the lantern and looked for it. But there wasn't no signs of any gold. Then the lantern got dry and went out, leaving me in the dark. I didn't know what to make of it. I went up the stairs and tried to open the door, but I couldn't budge it. Then I tried to dig my way out of the hole, but the old shovel I had broke and there I was. I'm an old man and pretty full of rheumatism, and staying down cellar all night has most finished me," concluded Hiram Duff, with a groan.

"Did the fellow say where he was going?" asked Sam, after a pause.

"Said he was going to get help, that's all, so

I couldn't rob him of that nugget. I don't know what to make of it. Might be he was a lunatic, eh?" went on the old miser, suddenly. "Maybe he run away from some asylum."

"Possibly," answered Sam, shortly. "Did he take anything, do you suppose?" he went on.

"Take anything? You mean steal anything?" cried Hiram Duff, and started back. The sandwich he had made for himself dropped fıom his hand. "I—I wonder if he did take anything," he muttered, and his eyes roved towards the other room of the cottage.

"Better take a look around, if you had anything of value," said Sam, and gave Songbird a meaning look.

With feeble steps the old miser walked out of the kitchen into what had been the sitting room of the cottage. As he was too feeble to sleep upstairs, Hiram Duff now used the apartment for a bedroom as well. He closed the door between the two rooms and the boys heard him rummaging around among his possessions. Then came a wild cry.

"It's gone! It's gone! My tin box is gone!"

"Your tin box?" repeated Songbird, as the old man threw open the door.

"Yes! yes! The fellow has robbed me! Oh, this is dreadful! What shall I do? I am a poor man! Oh, I'll have to go to the poor-house!" And the miser commenced to wring his hands.

"What did you have in the box?" questioned Sam.

"I had—some—er—some money, and some—er—jewelry," faltered Hiram Duff. He was a very secretive man naturally and it galled him to make the admission.

"How much money, Mr. Duff?"

"Oh, a—er—quite some. Oh, this is too bad! What shall I do? This will ruin me! Oh, where is that rascal? How can I catch him?" and the old man ran around the kitchen, staring at one thing and another, and at the boys.

"This must be Tom's work," whispered Sam to Songbird. "I wonder what I had best do about it?"

"Wait until you are sure it was Tom," advised the would-be poet.

Sam commenced to question the old miser regarding the looks of the fellow who had visited him. He soon became convinced that it must have been Tom. Clearly his brother must now be completely out of his mind.

"Poor, poor Tom," he sighed. "If he is going to act this way, what will he do next? I wish I could find him, and that Dick was here to help me to take care of him and clear up this mess."

"I don't know what I'm a-going to do," whined Hiram Duff. "I gotter find that box."

"How big a box was it?" questioned Sam.

"'Twasn't so very big—a fellow could put it in his pocket. But it had gold—I mean money—in it, and my dead wife's jewelry."

"How much money, Mr. Duff?"

"What business is that of yours?" demanded the miser, suspiciously.

"Why, I think—maybe I can help you get it back," stammered Sam. He grew red in the face. "To tell the plain truth, I think I know who that fellow was."

"Who?"

"Tell me what you lost first."

"Well, if you must know, that box had three hundred dollars in gold in it, besides the jewelry. That my wife got from her folks when they died, and they said it was wuth over a hundred dollars."

"Is that all?"

"Ain't that enough? Land sakes! I ain't no millionaire! That gold was a-going to keep me from the poorhouse." And Hiram Duff shook his head dolefully. He did not tell the young collegiates that he had an even ten thousand dollars in the banks. He had saved money all his life, denying himself and his wife almost the necessities of life.

"Do you suppose anybody else could have come in and taken the box?" said Songbird.

"What do you mean?"

"I mean, did anybody come in after that fellow left?"

"How should I know?—I was down cellar."

"Did you hear anybody?"

"I heard something. Maybe it was somebody, or maybe it was my sheep. They come up to the house sometimes.'

"I see."

"But what do you know about this?" demanded Hiram Duff, turning to Sam. "You said you might help me to git the money back."

"I'll tell you," said Sam, and related how his brother had disappeared and how the blow on the head seemed to have affected him.

"That's it! That's him! That's the man!" cried the old miser. "He did it! You catch him and git my money back!" he went on, excitedly.

"I'll certainly do my best to find him, Mr. Duff," answered Sam. "And if he really took your box you shall have what you lost back."

"Is he crazy, do you think?"

"He wouldn't do such a thing if he was in his right mind."

"Tom Rover is as honest as the day is long," declared Songbird. "If he really took your box he didn't know what he was doing."

"Well, he certainly did act queer," agreed Hiram Duff. "But that ain't here nor there. I want my box back, with all that's in it, and I'm going to have it. I guess I had better go to town and tell the police about this."

CHAPTER XIII

THE WESTERN EXPRESS

THE old miser was very much excited and began to pace the floor of his cottage.

"Yes, I better tell the police, that's what I better do," he muttered.

"There won't be any necessity to tell the police—if it was really my brother who did it," said Sam.

"Why not, I'd like to know?" challenged Hiram Duff. "He ain't no better'n other folks."

"If he took the box, I and my family will see to it that you are repaid for your loss, Mr. Duff," answered the youngest Rover.

"Humph! Do you guarantee that?" demanded the old miser, suspiciously.

"Yes."

"And you can take his word for it, sir," added Songbird. "The Rovers are well-known and wealthy, and they will do exactly as they promise."

"I've heard that name before. Didn't you

have some trouble with the railroad company?" asked Hiram Duff. "About a busted-up flying machine?"

"Yes," replied Sam.

"And got the best of that skinflint lawyer, Belright Fogg?"

"We made Mr. Fogg pay for the biplane, yes."

"I know all about it," chuckled Hiram Duff. "Served Fogg right. And he lost his job with the railroad company, too." The old man pursed up his lips. "Well, if you'll give me your word that you will settle with me I won't go to the police. But I want every cent that is coming to me, understand that."

"You'll get it—if my brother took the box," answered Sam. "But listen to me. First of all I want to find my brother. I think he ought to be under a doctor's care."

"He ought to be in an asylum," responded Hiram Duff, bluntly. It's dangerous to allow sech a feller at large."

"Maybe. We are going on a hunt for him right now," answered Sam. "I'll come back here, or you can come to see me at Brill. 'And don't worry, Mr. Duff,—you'll not lose a cent," added the youth, earnestly.

Luckily Hiram Duff had heard all about the

trouble the Rovers had had with the railroad lawyer, and had at the time also heard that Sam's family were wealthy and of high standing. This being so, he took matters far more calmly than would otherwise have been the case. But he wanted something in writing and Sam quickly wrote out a statement and signed it.

"Now we must get after my brother," said the youth. "Although you say you have no idea where he went?"

"No, I ain't got the least idee."

"Let us drive on towards Hoopville," suggested Songbird. "We can make inquiries along the way."

In a few minutes more the pair were on the way, Hiram Duff gazing after them anxiously.

"Don't forget to let me hear from you!" he called out.

"Songbird, this is terrible!" murmured Sam, as they drove on. "I wish Dick was here to advise me."

"He'll come as quickly as he can, don't worry about that, Sam. I only hope we catch Tom before he gets too far away."

About a mile was covered along the road leading to Hoopville, a small village, the single industry of which was the making of barrel hoops. Then they came to another farmhouse, where they saw a boy of fifteen sitting on a horse-block, whittling a stick.

"Hello, there!" called out Sam. "Say, I'm looking for a young fellow that passed here yesterday. Did you see anything of him? Here is his picture."

"Sure I saw him," answered the boy, after a glance at the photograph. "I drove him over to Morton's Junction."

"Drove him over to Morton's Junction?" repeated Sam. "When?"

"Yesterday afternoon. But we didn't git to the Junction till seven o'clock."

"Where did you go to?"

"What do you want to know for?" asked the boy, curiously.

"He is my brother and I want to find him, just as quickly as I can."

"Oh! Well, he wanted to catch a train. He just got it, too."

"What train?"

"The Western Express. He wouldn't have got it only it was about ten minutes late. He got aboard just as she started out from the depot."

Sam's heart sank at this news. Tom on the Western Express! For what place had he been bound?

"Did he say where he was going?" put in Songbird.

"To Chicago, I think. He talked to himself a good deal. Said something about Chicago and St. Paul and Seattle. I asked him if he was on business and he said he was going to pick up nuggets of gold. I guess he was poking fun at me," went on the boy, sheepishly. "But he paid me two dollars for driving him over," he added, with satisfaction.

"Did he have much money?" asked Sam. "Tell me all you know. I might as well tell tell you, that was my brother, and he is sick in his head, so that he doesn't know just what he is doing."

"Say, I thought he was queer—he had such a look out of his eyes, and talked so much to himself. He only had about ten dollars in bills. But he said he had some gold in his pocket, in a box. He didn't show it, though. He said he was on Bill Stiger's trail."

"Bill Stiger's trail," murmured Sam, and his mind went back to the night Tom had gone to see the moving picture drama entitled "Lost in the Ice Fields of Alaska." Bill Stiger had been the name of the villain in the play—the rascal who had robbed the hero of his golden nuggets.

"He didn't have no ticket," went on the

boy. "So he could get off the train anywhere."

"We must hurry to Morton's Junction and see if we can find out anything more," said Sam to his college chum. His face showed plainly how greatly he was worried.

The boy told them how to go and they made the best time possible, arriving at the Junction some time after noon. They found the depot master on the platform.

"I remember the fellow you mean," he said. "He got on the last car. Dunkirt, the conductor, helped him up. But I don't know where he went to. Maybe Dunkirt could tell you, when he gets back here."

"When will he be back?"

"He's off to-day and he'll be here on the one-thirty train. You can talk to him when he comes in, if you want to."

"I'll do it," answered Sam.

He and Songbird had an even hour to wait, and the latter suggested that they go to the Junction Hotel for dinner.

"Might as well eat, Sam," he said, kindly. "It won't help matters any to go hungry."

"I don't care much about eating, Songbird," was the answer. "But I'll go along and take a bite. I wish I knew just where

Tom had gone. I might telegraph ahead for him."

"Well, let us hope that conductor can tell you something."

With nothing to do but to wait, the boys took their time over the midday meal, and while doing this they had the team fed. Then they sauntered down to the depot to await the arrival of the man they wanted to interview. Presently the train came in and the depot master pointed out the conductor.

"Excuse me, but are you Mr. Dunkirt?" asked Sam.

"That's my handle," was the prompt reply.

"I am looking for the young man who jumped on your train just as it was leaving here yesterday."

"Ha! I thought somebody might be after that fellow!" exclaimed the conductor, quickly.

In a few words Sam explained as much of the situation as seemed necessary, the conductor listening with interest. He nodded his head several times.

"I thought he was a little bit off in his upper story," he said. "He talked rather wildly of going far away to get gold nuggets. He paid his fare to Chicago and that's as far as I carried him."

"What did he pay with?" asked Sam.

"He gave me a ten-dollar gold piece. He had quite a lot of gold with him."

"Did he say where he was going from Chicago?"

"Oh, yes, he had it all mapped out. He was going to St. Paul first and then straight west to Seattle. From there he was going to Alaska."

"Alaska!" cried Sam and Songbird, in a breath.

"That is what he said."

"What part of Alaska?" asked Sam, faintly.

"He didn't tell me and I didn't ask him. I rather thought he was kidding me, he acted so queer-like when he talked."

After this the conductor told all he could remember about Tom. He said that the youth had left the train at Chicago in a large crowd and that was the last he had seen of the youth.

"I'll send another telegram to Dick," said Sam to his chum.

"Why not telephone to Ashton first?" suggested the other. "There may be a telegram for you there."

"I'll do it," said Sam, and got the station master at Ashton on the wire as soon as possible.

"Yes, a telegram came in for you an hour

ago," was the answer, over the telephone wire. "I sent it up to Brill."

"Will you have the operator read it to me?" asked the youth.

"Sure. Hold the wire a minute."

Another connection was apparently made and Sam heard a different voice.

"Is this Samuel Rover?"

"Yes."

"Want that message from Richard Rover?"

"If you please."

"He says he is coming up to Ashton on the train that gets here at eleven-fifteen tonight."

"Is that all?"

"Yes."

"Very well. Thank you," and Sam hung up the receiver.

"What's the news, Sam?" questioned Songbird, and when told he looked relieved. "Dick will know what to do."

"I know what I am going to do, Songbird. I am going right back to Brill and get ready to follow Tom."

"I supposed you'd do that. I'd like to go with you."

"I know it. But that won't be necessary—if Dick goes with me." Sam drew a deep breath. "I—I guess I'd better stop at Hope on the way back and let the girls know how matters stand," he added, soberly.

"I can go up to-morrow and tell them, Sam."

"No, I'd rather tell them myself," answered the youngest Rover. He knew exactly how Nellie and Grace would feel when he broke the news to them.

It was a very sober and thoughtful pair of boys that got in the carriage and started back to Brill by the way of Hope Seminary. Sam was laying his plans how to follow Tom in his wild trip West and Songbird was wondering how he could be of assistance to the Rovers. Several times the would-be poet started to quote some original verse, but each time cut himself short.

Presently they came in sight of Hope, just as the girls were coming from their afternoon classes. They espied Nellie and Grace, and beckoned to them. Both came forward on a run.

"What is the news, Sam?" asked Nellie, quickly.

"It's not very good, Nellie," he said, kindly. "Tom has run away."

"Run away!" gasped the girl, and turned pale. "Oh, you don't mean it!"

"Where did he go to?" questioned Grace.

"To Chicago."

"And from there, so he told a train conductor, he was going to Seattle and then to Alaska," said Songbird. "Sam and Dick are going after him, just as soon as they can."

"To Alaska! Tom has gone to Alaska!" murmured Nellie, and then she turned and swayed, and the next moment fainted in Sam's arms.

CHAPTER XIV

DICK AND SAM IN CHICAGO

"GET some water, Songbird, quick!"

"Oh, Sam, shall I get some smelling salts!" cried Grace.

"I guess the water will do, Grace. Here, stand on this side, so those other girls can't see Nellie," went on the boy. "No use of letting them know everything."

Grace understood and she and Sam shielded Nellie and carried her to a campus bench. Then Songbird arrived with a cup of water from a well. Just as he handed it over, Nellie opened her eyes.

"Oh! I—I—what happened?" she murmured. "Oh, I remember now!" And a look of pain crossed her face.

"Take a drink of water, dear," said her sister, and held the cup. Nellie took a sip and then Grace bathed her forehead with some water poured on a handkerchief that Sam passed over. Soon the girl sat up straight.

"I—I'm all right now," she faltered. "It—it was such a—a shock. Oh, Sam, do you really think Tom is bound for Alaska?"

"It looks like it, Nellie," he answered. "I'll tell you all about it, if you'll walk down the road, away from those other students." And then, as they walked away slowly, Sam and Songbird told their story, the two girls hanging on their every word.

"It's awful, terrible!" murmured Grace. "Poor Tom, he must be clear out of his mind!"

"That's the only explanation," answered Sam. "He'd never do such a thing if he was in his right senses."

"Oh, but he may lose his mind entirely," gasped Nellie. "I've read of such cases in the newspapers. A person wanders off and forgets who he is, or where he came from, and all that! Supposing Tom went to Alaska and that happened to him! Why, we might never be able to find him!" And the tears began to course down Nellie's cheeks.

"We'll find him," answered Sam, sturdily. "Why, we've got to do it!"

"But Alaska is so big, Sam! And think of going out to those mining camps, and out in that snow and ice! Oh, I can't stand it!" And Nellie's tears started afresh.

"We'll have to catch him before he has a chance to leave St. Paul or Seattle," returned the youth.

"I think they had better telegraph ahead and set somebody on the watch," said Songbird. "It will cost money to send a description of Tom, but it may pay to do it."

"Yes, yes! Do that, Sam! Anything to find Tom!" pleaded Nellie.

"We'll do what we can, Nellie, you can be sure of that," was the reply.

The boys remained with the girls a short time longer and then took their departure.

"Take care of yourself, Sam," said Grace, on parting. "If you go West don't get into any trouble."

"I won't get into any more trouble than I can help," he replied. "But we are bound to find Tom and bring him back."

It was dark when the boys got back to Brill, and while Songbird prepared to go to supper, Sam hurried to the office of the head of the institution. He found Doctor Wallington pouring over some teacher's reports. He listened with a troubled face to what Sam had to tell and shook his head slowly.

"Too bad, Rover, and I sympathize with you and your family from the bottom of my heart.

Clearly that blow on the head has put your brother completely out of his mind. I am glad that Richard is coming to Ashton to aid you. What you had better do next is a problem."

"I think we'll send word West about Tom and then try to follow him," answered Sam. "That is why I came here—to notify you that I'd have to leave."

"I shall be sorry to lose you, Samuel. Let us hope that you'll be able to come back in a few days—and that Thomas's case will not prove as bad as we think. I agree that it is best for you to move at once, for there is no telling what your missing brother may do. Can I aid in any way?"

"You may cash a check for me—I may need some ready money,—if Dick doesn't happen to have enough with him."

"I'll do that with pleasure. Anything else?"

"I want to go to Ashton late this evening, to meet Dick. I'll take a suitcase with me."

"One of the men can drive you down. Will your brother come here?"

"Possibly. But both of us may stay in Ashton, to take the one o'clock train for Chicago. It stops on signal, you know."

"Yes. Very well. Anything else?"

"No, sir," answered Sam, and then he wrote

out the check and got his money. A little later, after a hasty supper, he started to pack his suitcase with such things as he thought he might need for the trip to Chicago.

He was in the midst of his labors when Songbird came in, followed by Spud, Stanley, Max and several others. All wanted to assist him, yet they could do little. Each was deeply sympathetic.

"It's too bad, Sam," said Spud. "I hope you catch Tom before he has a chance to leave Chicago. Why when a chap gets out of his mind there is no telling what he'll do, or where he'll go."

"Oxactly so," came from Max. "I knowed a man vonce dot goes his mind owid. He took an axe, and—vell neffer mind, Dom ton't do nuddings like dot anyvay," added the German-American student hastily, after a warning look from Songbird.

"I think that moving picture must have hit Tom hard," said Stanley. "It was so lifelike. He talked about it a great deal."

"Yes, he couldn't forget it. He even talked about it in his sleep," returned Sam. "He wanted to go out and get those nuggets of gold."

"Well, I'd like some nuggets myself," cried Spud. "But I am not going to the ice fields of

Alaska for 'em," he added, grimly, and this caused a faint smile to spread on some of the boys' faces.

Songbird had received permission to accompany Sam to Ashton, and at nine o'clock the youths were on the way, in a carriage driven by one of the college drivers. They went directly to the depot, there to await the arrival of the train that was to bring Dick.

It was a cold, disagreeable evening, with a promise of rain in the air. The boys were glad enough to go into the station, which was kept open for the coming of the late train.

"Can a fellow get on that one o'clock Chicago train from here?" asked Sam, of the ticket man.

"Yes, if he's got a ticket," was the reply. "I'll have to signal it to stop though."

"Well, I'll let you know about it as soon as I see my brother. He is coming in on the eleven-thirty."

It had begun to rain by the time the last-named train rolled in. Only three passengers got of, but one of them was Dick. He had a suitcase with him, and he fairly ran to meet Sam and Songbird.

"Any more news?" he demanded.

Sam related the particulars of what had occurred. In the meantime the train had gone on and the station was deserted by all but the ticket man.

"Going to lock up now," he said to the boys, who had gathered in the station, out of the rain.

"Wait just one minute please," pleaded Sam.

"Here, go out and get some cigars for yourself," added Dick, and passed over a quarter.

"Thanks, I will," returned the ticket man, and walked off to an all-night resort not far from the station.

"I don't see anything to do but to follow Tom to Chicago," said Dick. "We might send a telegram to the authorities, but I can't see how it would do any good. They don't know him, and in a big city like that it is hard enough to find a fellow when he is well-known. If we take that one o'clock train we'll be in Chicago by morning, and I'd rather look around myself than trust the police to do it."

"All right, I came prepared for the trip," answered Sam, and pointed to his suitcase.

When the station man came back they purchased two tickets for Chicago and the man set out his lantern to signal the express. Then Songbird said good-bye, wishing them all kinds of good luck, and rode back to Brill.

"Sam, this is simply terrible," observed the big brother, as he paced the depot platform, the station master having gone away. "I never thought such a thing as this would come to Tom."

"Neither did I, Dick. Nellie is all broke up over it, too."

"Naturally."

"Did you send word home? I didn't."

"No, I didn't want to worry the folks until the last minute. But Dora knows, and so does Mrs. Stanhope."

"What about Dad's business, Dick? Can you get away from it?"

"I can't get away any too easily, Sam. Things are in a fearful snarl. But I telephoned to Mr. Powell, the lawyer, to look after matters during my absence. I think we've got those brokers under our thumb—at least I hope so. But if we haven't, we stand to lose a bunch of money."

"How much?"

"Twenty or thirty thousand dollars."

"That's too bad. If you think you ought to go back, I might look for Tom alone."

"Don't you dare to mention such a thing, Sam. I think more of Tom than I do of twice that amount of money—and so do you and the rest of the family. Our whole duty is to find Tom, and do it, too, before he gets into more mischief, or gets hurt," concluded the oldest Rover.

Promptly on time the night express bound west came along. It seldom stopped at Brill and the conductor gazed curiously at the two youths as they got aboard. Then the lantern was extinguished and set aside, and the heavy train rolled on.

Fortunately travel was light that night, so the lads had no trouble in getting a section of a sleeper from the Pullman porter. They had only the lower berth made up, and on that laid down, to talk matters over and get some sleep.

"Yes, it must have been that moving picture that set Tom off," said Dick, during the course of the conversation. "And that gives us something like a clue to work on. The main scenes took place in Alaska, and he may be just topsy-turvy enough in his mind to want to find those places. Talking about golden nuggets, and about being on the trail of Bill Stiger, looks like it, anyway."

"I think so myself, Dick. But his mind may change and he may go to Mexico, or Europe," and Sam sighed deeply.

Neither of the boys slept much and both were up almost as early as anybody on the train. More to pass the time than because they felt hungry, they went into the dining car for breakfast.

At last the train rolled into the suburbs of the great city of the lakes and finally came to a stop at the big depot. The youths took up their suitcases and filed out with the other passengers.

"Have you any idea where we ought to look first?" asked Sam.

"I think we may as well leave our bags on check at this depot and look around here," was the answer. "Tom started from here and maybe we'll be lucky enough to meet somebody who saw and remembered him."

Having checked the suitcases, the Rovers started in earnest, asking the men at the news stand and in the smoking room and at the lunch counter and restaurant. Then they questioned the taxicab drivers, and even some of the newsboys and bootblacks.

"It looks almost hopeless," said Sam, at last.

"Not yet," returned Dick. "We haven't struck the most important people yet. Funny we didn't think of them first."

"Whom do you mean?"

"The ticket sellers. Let me have that photo of Tom and we'll see if any of them remember him."

From one ticket window they went to another,

until they reached an elderly man, who gazed at the photograph with interest.

"Yes, I remember that young man," he said, slowly. "He was here yesterday afternoon."

"Did he buy a railroad ticket?"

"He did."

"Where to?"

"Seattle."

"Can you remember on what train?" asked Sam.

"Sure. I had to hurry for him, for he took the four-ten train, by way of St. Paul," was the reply.

CHAPTER XV

BOUND WEST

"WELL, Sam we have done all we can do for the present."

"That's right, Dick."

"Whether it will do any good or not remains to be seen," and Dick gave a long-drawn sigh and leaned back in the sleeping car seat he occupied.

It was about three hours later and in that time the Rover boys had been very busy.

Following the announcement of the ticket seller that Tom had taken a train for Seattle by way of St. Paul, the Rovers had sent a telegram to the conductor of the train, asking him to look out for Tom and have him detained. They had procured accommodations on the train they were now on, and had so notified the railroad official, so he would know where to address them, provided the missing one was found. They had also sent a telegram to the folks at home and another to the girls at Hope.

"Perhaps we'll get word when we reach St. Paul," said Sam. "For all we know Tom may be there, awaiting our arrival."

"I sincerely hope so, Sam. I'm sure I don't want to go away out to the Pacific coast for him."

"It's too bad Tom didn't buy one of those railroad tickets that a fellow has to sign," observed Sam. "If he had done that, it would be easy to find him."

"That's true."

The train they were on was an express, making but few stops and would reach St. Paul late in the evening. It was only about three-quarters filled, so the Rovers had had no difficulty in getting a section of a sleeper. Whether they would go further than St. Paul was, however, as yet a problem.

"Next stop Milwaukee!" was the cry, and soon the train rolled into that city. Anxiously the two brothers looked out and saw one of the trainmen take several telegrams from a man on the platform. After the train had started again the trainman came through the train.

"Telegrams for Miss Baker, Mr. Josephs and Mr. Rover!" he called out.

"Here you are!" cried Sam, eagerly. "Rover." And the telegram was passed over. Hastily the envelope was torn open and the contents scanned. The boys looked at each other blankly. The telegram read as follows:

"No young man answering to name Tom Rover on this train. Will watch passengers closely as instructed.

"FOLSOM, *Conductor.*"

"What do you make of this, Dick. Maybe Tom didn't use that ticket after he bought it," gasped Sam.

"But that ticket seller saw him rush for the gate. He must have gone on the train, Sam. He probably didn't answer to his name because if he is out of his mind he has forgotten what his real name is. And so long as he keeps quiet the trainmen won't suspect anything wrong with him."

"Perhaps we'll get another telegram at St. Paul."

"I hope so."

On and on rolled the train through the afternoon, coming presently to the shore of the upper Mississippi, with its wide stretches of marshland and its dead trees. It was not an inviting scene, and the two Rovers were glad enough, when the time came, to turn from it and go to the diner for dinner.

There was to be a stop of ten minutes at St.

Paul and in that time the boys must make up their minds whether they were going to continue on that train or not. If they laid over, several more hours of precious time would be lost.

It was well towards midnight when the train reached St. Paul and a number of sleepy passengers got off and others got on. Dick and Sam waited impatiently for a messenger to appear. The telegram was there, sure enough, and this time it carried more interesting information.

"Queer-acting young man found, but says his name is Paul Haverlock. Says he is bound for Alaska. Wire positive instructions, as I can take no risks.

"FOLSOM, *Conductor.*"

"It must be Tom!" cried Sam.

"But that name, Paul Haverlock," mused Dick. "Where did he get that?"

"Why, I remember, Dick! In that moving picture the hero was called Paul Haverlock. His name was on the letters they showed on the screen. Tom must have remembered it, just as he remembered the name of the villain, Bill Stiger!"

"I see. Then this Paul Haverlock must really

be Tom," returned Dick. "Now to have him stopped. I wonder where that other train is now?"

They found out that the other train was then in the vicinity of Livingston, the junction point for Yellowstone Park. From there it was bound for Helena, Spokane, and then to Seattle direct.

"We'll telegraph again, and keep right on this train," said Dick, and this was done.

If the two youths had slept but little the night before, they were even more restless this night. And yet they realized that Folsom, the conductor of the other train, would not be likely to arouse Tom if he had gone to bed.

"He won't take the chance," said Dick. "Remember, he isn't sure of what he is doing, and all railroad men like to keep out of trouble. If he made a mistake, the passenger might sue the railroad company for big damages, and get them."

"If only we could catch up to Tom!" sighed Sam.

"That is impossible, Sam, because he is on an express, just as we are. As it is, he'll gain on us when he gets to Spokane, for he will go through without waiting, while we'll either have to lay over or go by some other route that is much longer."

As there seemed nothing more to do just then they at last went to sleep, and did not rouse up again until it was broad daylight.

They immediately asked for further news, but were informed that none had come in. Nor did any word come in all that forenoon.

"This suspense is fierce," was Dick's remark, at last. "That conductor is either asleep or has given up the search. I wish I knew of some first-class detective on the other end of the line who could take up the case for us."

"We'd know somebody if Tom was bound for San Francisco," returned his brother. "But I don't know a soul in Seattle—oh, yes, I do!" he suddenly shouted.

"Who, Sam?"

"A fellow named Jim Hendricks. He is a cousin of Stanley Browne, and also a cousin to Larry Colby, who went to Putnam Hall with us. He was at Brill once, for a week, and I got pretty well acquainted with him."

"Why, yes, I remember him. He and I used to talk about what Larry and I did at Putnam Hall. But is he in Seattle now, and have you his address?"

"I think I have his address. Wait, I'll look," and Sam pulled a little notebook out of his pocket. "He asked me to write to him some time, but I never did more than mail him a postal. Yes, here is the address."

"Do you think he would help us, if he was home?"

"Sure I do. He got acquainted with Tom, and he knew what chums Tom and Larry were at the Hall."

"Then we might telegraph him. It won't do any harm anyway."

A rather long telegram was prepared and sent from the next station at which the train stopped. There the youths hoped for another message from Folsom the conductor, but none came.

Slowly the hours dragged by, the express thundering along in the meanwhile on its journey westward. They stopped at Livingston, and there many passengers got off, bound for a trip through that great natural wonderland, Yellowstone Park. At Helena they heard from Folsom again. This time the message was one full of mystery.

"Cannot find Paul Haverlock anywhere. So far as known, he did not leave train at any station. We are very much crowded, account special excursion, and break down of Number 126. Attached two extra cars. He may be hiding among new passengers. I can do no more."

"I think I can explain this," said the conductor of the train, when Dick showed him the telegram. "Number 126, the train just ahead of Number 182, the one your brother is on, broke down. Now, the second train is carrying two cars of the other train, and most likely all of the other train's passengers. So Folsom is having his hands full with his extra duties. In the meantime your brother has disappeared, probably in the crowd of extra passengers."

"If he didn't jump off the train," sighed Sam.

"Would he do that?" asked the railroad man.

"I don't know. A fellow who is out of his mind is liable to do anything."

"That is true."

The train was now in the midst of the Rocky Mountains, but the Rovers had no heart to look at the scenery.

"Oh, if only we get some sort of encouraging word at Spokane!" sighed Sam.

"We ought to hear from Jim Hendricks," answered Dick. "That is, if he is home and got our message." They knew that the Hendricks family were rich and that Jim had a great deal of time to himself.

At Spokane they left the train, for they did not want to go down to Portland, whither it was bound. They asked at the telegraph office for a

message and one was handed over to them.
"This is something like it!" cried Dick, as he read it aloud. It ran as follows:

"My sincere sympathy. I remember Tom well and will be on the watch for him. Will meet you on your arrival.

"JAMES V. HENDRICKS."

"Well, that's one word of encouragement," said Sam. "Good for Jim! I thought he'd help us."

"If he only got the message in time to catch Tom," returned his brother. "We were rather late in getting it to him, remember."

"We'll have to hope for the best."

While the boys were waiting around Spokane, for the train to take them to Seattle, they fell in with a commercial drummer who said he was waiting for a companion with some sample cases. He was a kindly-looking man and during the course of his conversation let slip the news that he had been on the train Tom had taken.

"Perhaps you can give us some information," cried Dick. "We are trying to catch a young man who was on that train," and he gave a few of the particulars.

"Well! well!" cried the commercial drummer. "To be sure I met that fellow. The way I noticed him was because he acted so queer. He didn't want to sit still, but kept walking up and down the aisle and from one car to another. I saw the conductor talk to him once or twice, too."

"Where did he go?" questioned Sam.

"Well, you know the train ahead of ours broke down and we hooked fast to some of the cars. When this was done a lot of new passengers got in our cars, and there was something of a mix-up. I saw the fellow go into one of the cars from the other train, and that's the last I did see of him."

"And that train went right through to Seattle?" asked Dick.

"Yes. That is, unless they had more trouble on the line. And by the way, did you hear of what happened on the trip from St. Paul? A lady lost her handbag containing jewelry to the value of ten thousand dollars."

CHAPTER XVI

THE ROVER BOYS IN SEATTLE

SAM and Dick looked at each other in new alarm. They remembered only too well what had occurred at Hiram Duff's cottage. Was it possible that Tom had seen the lady's jewels and taken them? In his unbalanced state of mind he was liable to do anything.

"She had the jewels in her handbag?" questioned Dick.

"Yes, a little black affair—so she told the conductor. When she discovered that it was gone she was almost crazy. She said some of the jewelry belonged to her mother, who was with her."

"Was this in your car?"

"Yes, up at the other end from where I sat, though." And the commercial drummer grinned. "Oh, I had nothing to do with it," he added, lightly.

"I didn't suppose you had," returned Dick. "But where was this other fellow—the one I think was my brother—at this time?"

"Why, he sat up near the other end, too—about two seats from the lady. He said, the same as did everybody on the car, that he hadn't seen the bag or the jewels. The conductor and the porter made a long search, but nothing came of it. The lady was wild, and said she would get her husband to sue the company for her loss. She had the conductor worried, I can tell you."

"And that's why he lost interest in helping us," murmured Dick. "He certainly had his hands full, with that train breakdown and the missing jewels, and looking for Tom."

"Who sat next to the lady?" asked Sam.

"Her mother, a very old woman."

"And was that young man we mentioned next?"

"Yes."

"Couldn't they find any trace of the bag at all?"

"Not a thing. It was mighty queer, and the woman made it worse by being so excited. She could hardly tell when she had seen the bag last, or where. First she said she had had it in her lap and then she said she guessed she had put it on a hook with her coat."

"What did they do about it?"

"I don't know, for I got off here, while the

lady and her mother went through to Seattle," answered the drummer.

The commercial man could tell but little more of importance to the Rovers, and presently, when his companion came with the sample cases, he went away.

"Dick, do you think Tom took that lady's handbag with the jewels?" asked Sam, when the two were by themselves.

"Sam, I don't know what to think," was the discouraging reply. "I only know one thing—the quicker we locate Tom and put him in some safe place, the better."

"Do you—you think his mind is affected for good—I mean for always?"

"Let us hope not. Why, it would be terrible to have to keep him in an asylum for the rest of his life! It would just about kill father. And think of Nellie."

"It certainly is the worst thing that ever happened!" muttered Sam. "It's worse than our trouble with Dan Baxter, Lew Flapp, or with Sobber and those brokers, and old Crabtree."

"So it is."

When the train for Seattle finally came in they got abroad. It was so crowded that they had to take seats in a day coach. But this they did not mind. They would have ridden on a freight train, could they have gotten to Seattle faster thereby.

Hour after hour passed slowly. The boys could not settle down to read, and they had little appetite for their meals. They caught a little sleep in their seats, and were ready to leave the train the moment the conductor called out that they were approaching Seattle.

"I see Jim Hendricks!" cried Sam, as he looked out of a window.

"Is Tom with him?" queried his brother.

"No, he is alone."

In a minute more they were out of the train, suitcases in hand, and shaking hands with the cousin of Stanley and Larry. Jim Hendricks' usually jolly face showed his deep concern.

"I've got bad news for you," he said. "That train Tom was on got here before I did, and so I didn't have a chance to stop him. I've been making some inquiries though, and I am pretty certain he reached this place. One man who was on the train told me he had met a young fellow who said he was bound for Alaska to find some nuggets of gold. He wanted to know about the ships that sailed for Sitka and Juneau, and the man told him what he knew. He said the young fellow went off in the direction of the shipping offices."

"Oh, Dick! we must get after him at once!" cried Sam.

"That's it, Sam." Dick turned to Jim Hendricks. "Will you show us where they are? We can go in a taxicab."

"I've got our auto outside—we can go in that, and you may as well bring your baggage along," continued the Seattle young man. "If you have to remain in town, I want you to stay at our house."

"Thanks, that's kind of you," answered Dick.

Jim led the way outside, to where stood a handsome six-cylinder touring car. "I don't know when the steamers sail, but we can soon find out," he said, and directed the chauffeur where to go.

They were soon passing through the streets of Seattle, a well-built up city where much business is done. As many of my young readers must know, Seattle is located on Puget Sound, one of the great natural gateways to the Pacific Ocean. Just south of it is Tacoma, also a city of importance.

The ride to the first of the shipping offices did not take long, and going inside Dick made some inquiries of the clerk at the desk.

"Don't remember any such man," said the clerk.

"When is your next sailing?"

"Day after to-morrow. Want to book for the passage?"

"Perhaps. I don't know yet."

"Better make up your mind pretty quick. We have only a few berths left," went on the clerk.

"We are looking for a certain young man who was bound for Alaska," went on Dick, producing Tom's photograph. "Have you seen anything of him?"

The clerk gave a glance at the photograph and started.

"Well, that's strange!" he cried.

"You saw him?" put in Sam, eagerly.

"I sure did. Did you want to meet him?"

"Very much."

"Well, I'm sorry, but I don't see how you are going to do it. His name was, let me see—Haverlock, I believe."

"That's the name he was traveling under," answered Dick, giving his brother a nudge in the ribs.

"Wasn't his own then?" and the clerk became interested.

"No, it's an assumed name. I might as well tell you, the young man isn't all here," and Dick touched his forehead.

"I thought that might be it—he acted so

queerly. But he got his ticket for the other boat. You see it was this way: He came in here just as I was talking to a man who had purchased a ticket for the other boat and wanted to stay in Seattle another week. The man wanted me to exchange the ticket or give him his money back. While we were discussing the matter, this Haverlock, or whatever his name is, came in. He listened for a minute and then said he'd take the ticket and glad of the chance, for he said he was in a mighty hurry to get some nuggets of gold. So the man transferred the ticket to him, and that was the last I saw of the young fellow."

"When did that other boat sail?" asked Sam.

"Last night, at nine o'clock."

"Last night!" cried Dick. "Then he certainly must have rushed matters!" He looked at Jim Hendricks. "What can we do next, do you suppose?"

"You might send a wireless to the steamship," was the suggestion. "If he's under the name of Haverlock they ought to be able to hold him. Where did the steamer sail for?" Jim went on, to the clerk.

"For Ketchikan, Juneau, Skagway, and all the regular ports."

"She carries a wireless?" asked Sam.

"Certainly. You can send a message from here if you wish. We can telephone it over to the wireless station."

"Let's do it!" burst out Sam. "The quicker somebody takes charge of poor Tom the better!"

"You're right," answered Dick. He wiped his forehead with his handkerchief. "What a pity we didn't get here sooner, or that Tom wasn't delayed!"

Then he and Sam got a blank and started to write out the wireless message that might put those on board the steamer on the track of Tom.

CHAPTER XVII

OFF FOR ALASKA

"WHAT steamer was that?" questioned Dick and the clerk told him.

"I suppose we had better address the captain," said Sam. "Now, the question is, What shall we say?"

"We'll give Tom's assumed name and a short description of him, and ask that he be held for us at one of the ports," said Dick. "I don't know what else to do."

"I don't think the captain will hold the young man on your say-so," said the clerk, on being questioned. "He would be afraid of getting into trouble with the authorities. You had better get the police to make the request."

"The trouble is, we don't want to make this too public," explained Dick. "We'd rather keep it quiet. I'll risk the personal message to the captain."

"I'll sign the message with you," said Jim

Hendricks. "Maybe the captain will know our family, at least by reputation."

"Who are you, if I may ask?" came from the clerk, curiously.

"I am James Hendricks, and my father is Colonel Wilby Hendricks."

"Oh, yes, I guess Captain Dwight knows of your father. Your name will carry weight with him," added the clerk, for he knew that the colonel was well-known and was rich.

After considerable trouble the message was made out and telephoned at once to the wireless station. This accomplished, there was nothing to do but to wait for an answer.

"When is the next sailing for Alaskan ports?" asked Dick.

"Our sailing, as I told you before, is day after to-morrow. But one of the other lines has a sailing to-morrow, at nine P. M."

"They all seem to sail at nine o'clock at night," mused Sam.

"Yes, that is the usual hour," answered the clerk.

"Well, if we have to, we can take that boat at nine o'clock to-morrow night," remarked Dick."

"Provided you can get accommodations," said the clerk.

"Oh, we'll get aboard somehow—if we really have to go."

Jim Hendricks insisted that the Rovers ride up to his house with him, and away sped the touring car for the most fashionable quarter of Seattle. Here the Hendricks had a beautiful mansion, and here the newcomers were cordially greeted by Mrs. Hendricks, the colonel being out of the city on business.

"You've just got to make yourselves at home," said Jim. "It won't do a bit of good to fret so much. You are bound to get hold of poor Tom sooner or later, and I can't see that this trip to Alaska is going to hurt him any. It may do him good."

"But he may wander away and we may lose all track of him," answered Sam. "I've heard of persons disappearing like that."

The Hendricks did all in their power to make the Rovers feel at home. Sam and Dick were utterly worn out and took a brief rest. After that came an elaborate meal, served in the Hendricks' spacious dining room.

The telephone rang several times, but they were only local messages, of no importance to the Rover boys. But then came another message that filled them with interest, being from the wireless office.

"It's from Captain Dwight," explained Jim, who took the message down. "Too bad," he murmured.

"What does he say?" demanaded Sam and Dick, in a breath.

"He can't find anybody by the name of Paul Haverlock, nor can he find any passenger answering to the description you gave him of Tom. He says, 'Too many answering your general description,' which means that he can't pick Tom out, even if he is on board."

"Tom must have changed his name again," said Sam. "Most likely he gives any name that happens to come into his head."

"But he ought to be on the steamer's list of passengers."

"That's true. I can't understand it."

For a long time the Rover boys talked the matter over. Had Tom really gone to Alaska?

"We had better make some inquiries at the dock from which that steamer sailed," said Dick. "Maybe we'll meet somebody who will remember Tom."

The next morning found them at the dock, Jim going with them. All sorts of men and boys were interviewed, and at last they met a taxicab driver who had carried Tom from the railroad station. He recognized the photograph at once.

"Yes, I took him from the depot to the shipping office, and then carried his handbag to the steamer," said the taxicab driver. "He was a fine young man," he added.

"Maybe he tipped you pretty good," ventured Dick, with a faint smile.

"He sure did—gave me fare and a dollar over."

"And you are dead sure he got on the steamer?" insisted Sam.

"I am. He was almost the last passenger on board and I am sure he didn't come ashore again."

"Then he must have gone to Alaska," said Dick.

The youths had already learned that the ticket Tom had purchased had been for Skagway. At that point, so the agent had told them, a connection could be made for the White Pass and Yukon Route.

"That's the way Tom would go—if he wanted to get up to where that moving picture was taken," said Dick. "That's the land of gold—and also ice and snow."

"I guess the best thing we can do, Dick, is to get to Juneau and Skagway as soon as we can."

"It would seem so, Sam. It's a pretty long journey."

"So it is, but what else is there to do? We don't want poor Tom to become hopelessly lost, and in such a far-away country as that."

"If the travel wasn't so awfully heavy we'd have a better chance to locate Tom," went on Dick. "But with the steamers so loaded it is pretty hard to find anybody just by a description."

As the boys had both left Ashton in a hurry they had but few things with them. In the Hendricks car they traveled around Seattle, purchasing such things as they needed.

"I don't suppose Tom has much clothing," said Sam. "Poor fellow, I do hope he doesn't go away up North where it is so cold!"

"I've got to send some word home and to New York," said Dick, after the shopping was over.

"Dick, can you really spare the time to go to Alaska?" questioned his brother. "If you can't, I could go alone."

"I think it is best for us to go together, Sam. I imagine we are going to have our hands full, too. As for Dad's business, it will have to wait, that's all. I think I can trust Mr. Powell to do the right thing. The worst of the whole business is, this is going to worry Dad and Aunt Martha and Uncle Randolph a great deal. But that can't be helped."

At last came the time for the steamer to leave. The brothers had been fortunate in getting a stateroom together. It was not a very desirable room, but it was much better than nothing. And they would have gone, "if they had to sleep on the anchor," as Sam expressed it.

Jim Hendricks came down to see them off. He shook hands cordially on parting.

"I'm sure I wish you the best of luck," he said. "And I'll write to your chums at Brill, telling them of what is taking place."

Slowly the big steamer left the harbor and turned her bow towards the North. It was dark, so but little outside of the twinkling lights of the city could be seen. Yet the Rovers remained on deck for over an hour, for neither felt like turning in.

They noticed that the passengers were quite a mixed set. Many were mere tourists, taking a round trip to Alaska for sight seeing. Others were Alaskan merchants and traders, who had been "down to the States" on business. Mixed in with the crowd were many men, young and middle-aged, bound for the North to try their luck in the gold fields. The great rush to the Klondyke was a thing of the past, but new gold fields were being opened continually.

The boys were on their way to their stateroom when they came suddenly face to face with a burly man who wore a heavy beard and moustache. The man was about to pass them when he suddenly stopped short, stared at Dick and then at Sam, and caught each by the arm.

"Say, am I dreamin', or is this the Rovers!" he gasped.

"We are the Rovers, yes," answered Dick, and he gave the burly man a closer look. "And this is Jack Wumble, I believe," he added.

"Jack Wumble!" cried Sam. "Really!"

"Put her thar! Put her thar!" cried the man, and took hold of the hand of each at once. "Ain't this great! Whar ye bound now anyhow? Goin' to locate another mine—like thet one we found out in Colorady?"

"No, we are not looking for a mine this trip," answered Dick. "We are on the trail of something far more important."

"More important than a gold mine?" demanded Jack Wumble, his eyes opening widely.

"Yes. We are on the trail of my brother Tom, who is out of his mind and has wandered away."

"Hoss pistols an' rattlesnakes! Ye don't tell me! Well, if Tom is missin' count me in on the hunt fer him," was the quick and earnest response.

CHAPTER XVIII

AT JUNEAU AND SKAGWAY

JACK WUMBLE was an old miner and prospector, a man the boys had met years before in Colorado, when they went to that section of our country to locate a mine belonging to their father. As related in detail in "The Rover Boys Out West," Wumble had been of great assistance to them and he knew them all well. He had, after numerous stirring adventures, located a claim for himself, which, at the time, paid very well. Lately, however, the Rovers had not heard from him, and they had often wondered what had become of the man.

"You're a sight fer sore eyes, so ye are!" cried Jack Wumble, slapping each on the shoulder. "I never dreamed o' seein' ye in this out o' the way corner o' the country."

"We didn't expect to come here either, up to a few days ago," answered Sam.

"Maybe ye better tell me the story," suggested the old miner. "If I kin help ye I will."

"Come on to the cabin," suggested Dick, and led the way. They sat down on a corner seat, and there the Rovers told their story, withholding nothing, for they knew they could trust Jack Wumble in every particular.

"Gosh all hemlock! Sounds like one of them theatre plays I see in 'Frisco," was the old miner's comment. "To think Tom would wander away in thet fashion! 'Tain't no wonder ye are scart to deth! I'd be scart myself, thinkin' he might jump overboard, or sumthin' like thet. He ought to be put in an asylum."

After that Jack Wumble told his own story. He said his claim in Colorado had gradually petered out, and then he had tried his fortunes in various other places, gradually winding up in the Klondyke. There he had struck what he hoped would prove a bonanza.

"I've been down to the States buying some machinery an' some supplies," he added. "They are coming up on a freight boat next week. I find I can do better to go to the States fer things than to buy in Alaska."

"Have you taken any gold out of your claim yet?" questioned Sam, with interest.

Jack Wumble looked around, to make certain that nobody was listening but the Rovers.

"Don't ye tell nobody," he whispered. "I

THE JOURNEY TO ALASKA WAS FULL OF INTEREST TO THE BOYS.

The Rover Boys in Alaska *Page* 181

took out about two thousand dollars, in nuggets an' dust, in less'n ten days!"

"Fine!" returned Dick, and Sam nodded. "I hope you keep it up."

"It's the machinery is goin' to tell the tale," returned Jack Wumble. "I can't do much more by hand."

"Are you working the mine alone?" asked Sam.

"Fer the present. When I came away I left the claim in charge o' a miner named Allison—Tim Allison. But I told him not to do any diggin'—just keep his eyes on things. When there is any diggin' to be done I want to be on hand."

Wumble was bound for Skagway, where he said his machinery and supplies would be sent. He knew that section of Alaska thoroughly, and said he would show the lads where to go and what to do.

"Things is changin' mightily up there every day," he remarked. "They are dredgin' channels an' buildin' railroads, and making all kinds o' roads. Go there one year an' the next ye won't 'most know the place, it will look so different."

"Well, they are developing all parts of the country," answered Dick.

"Maybe; but nuthin' to wot they're doin' in Alaska," answered the old miner.

The three sat up for half an hour longer, talking matters over. Of course Jack Wumble wanted to know about Mr. Rover, and was sorry to learn that the boys' father was not well. He could hardly believe that Dick was married.

"Why, it don't seem like no time since you an' your brothers came out to Colorady to locate thet mine," he remarked.

There was a little wind, but otherwise the night was calm. Now that they could do no more for the present, the Rovers realized how tired they were, and once in their berths both went sound asleep. Nor did they rouse up until well into the morning. The sleep did them a world of good, and when they dressed and went to breakfast they felt quite like themselves once more.

"If we didn't have to worry about Tom, I could enjoy this trip immensely," remarked Sam.

Jack Wumble had already satisfied his hunger, for he was an early riser. After breakfast all sat on the deck, and the old miner related some of his experiences while prospecting in various localities, and the boys told how they had finished up at Putnam Hall and gone to Brill.

"I can't hardly believe thet Dan Baxter has

reformed," said Wumble, shaking his head slowly. "I allers put him an' his father down fer bad eggs."

"Well, they were pretty bad at one time," answered Dick. "But Dan found out that it didn't pay to be bad. And his father is old and, I guess, well satisfied to behave himself and take it easy."

"Mr. Baxter might have been a wealthy man if he had done things on the level," returned the old miner.

The journey up the coast of Canada to the lower point of Alaska was full of interest to the boys. In due course of time, the bow of the steamer was turned into Chatham Strait, and soon they were running past Admiralty Island.

Both Sam and Dick had expected to see quite a city at Juneau, and they were disappointed when they beheld only a scattered town, lying on a strip of land, bound on one side by what is called the Lynn Canal and on the other by the mouth of the Taku River. In the distance were some high mountains, which the boys looked at with interest.

Fortunately the steamer was to remain at Juneau for two hours, and in that time the Rovers hoped to make certain whether or not Tom had landed there. They lost no time in getting ashore, and Jack Wumble went with them.

At first there was so much confusion at the dock that the youths could learn little or nothing. But as the crowd cleared away they were enabled to make some inquiries of officials and others. But nobody had seen Tom, or knew anything about him.

"I think he must have remained on the steamer," said Sam. "If he was after those nuggets he'd want to get right up into the land of gold."

"Thet's the way I reason it out," put in Jack Wumble. "Better stick to the trip, lads. I think ye'll be able to learn somethin' in Skagway."

So when the steamer left the dock they were on board.

The trip to Skagway was a decidedly interesting one, and the youths listened closely to all the old miner had to tell them about the country and its inhabitants.

"It's changin' amazingly fast," said Jack Wumble. "They are clearin' out ship channels an' buildin' railroads, and towns spring up like magic. Now whar I'm located—a place called Black Run—thar wasn't a house thar three years ago. Now we got a store an' a dozen shacks, an' more buildin' every day! I tell you, I think

Alaska is one o' the greatest countries in the world!"

There was a greater bustle and confusion than ever when the steamer tied up at Skagway. Here a connection can be made with the White Pass and Yukon route, and other routes. About ten miles away, up the Lynn Canal, was Dyea, also a town of importance.

The boys followed Jack Wumble ashore and waited until some of the bustle and confusion was over, and then commenced a systematic hunt for Tom.

The hunt lasted until nearly midnight, and then, utterly worn out, the Rovers and the old miner had to give it up. They had met just one man who remembered having seen a person who looked like Tom on the steamer, and who said the fellow had landed at Skagway. But where the unknown had gone the man could not say.

"Yes, that's the fellow," said the man, when shown Tom's photograph. "But he didn't look quite as nice as that. He looked—well, wild like."

"He is wild," answered Dick. "That is why we want to find him."

Jack Wumble knew of a fairly good hotel, and the three put up there for the night. The boys were so tired they slept "like logs," as

Dick said afterwards. But they were up bright and early, along with the old miner, and directly after breakfast set out on another search for Tom.

"I hate to waste your time, Jack," said Dick, to Wumble. "So if you want to go ahead——"

"Stop right thar, Dick!" cried the old miner. "I ain't in sech an all-fired hurry I can't try to do ye a good turn. I like Tom, an' I'm going to stay with ye fer a few days an' see if we can't locate him." And thus the matter was settled.

Two days were spent in Skagway and Dyea hunting for the missing one. Late in the afternoon of the second day the boys and the old miner separated, to make inquiries in different places.

Sam and Dick came back to the hotel at supper time much discouraged, having heard nothing to their advantage. Half an hour later Jack Wumble came in, his face showing his excitement.

"I've got on the trail!" he cried. "Come on, we're goin' to git after Tom right away!"

CHAPTER XIX

FROM ONE CLUE TO ANOTHER

"WHAT have you learned, Jack?"

"When did he leave here?"

"Is he all right?"

"I'm ready to go after him right now."

Such were the words that came from the Rover boys after Jack Wumble had announced that he had located their missing brother.

"We ain't got no time to spare," cried the old miner. "Let us pay our bill here an' git out, an' I'll tell ye all I know while we are on the way."

The lads lost no time in packing up as directed, and Dick settled at the hotel desk. Jack Wumble led the way down to the docks and ordered them into a small river boat.

"This here ain't no regular boat," he explained. "But I've hired passage on her, so it's all right. We'll save fourteen hours by not waitin' fer the regular boat."

"But where are we going, Jack?" questioned Dick.

"To a jumpin'-off place called Lindy Falls. That is whar the party Tom was with was goin' to start from."

Soon the boat, a large craft of its kind, was on the way up the river. As they sped along, the boys and the old miner drew into a corner of the cabin and Jack Wumble told his story.

"By the merest accident I fell in with a man named Rabig I used to know in 'Frisco," said the old miner. "He's interested in the Golden Sunset mine an' the Beggar's Chance. Well, I told Rabig about you an' Tom an' he got interested an' asked me how Tom looked an' I told him. Then he told about how he fell in with Tom on board thet steamer an' how Tom had told him he was bound fer the Lion Head gold fields. He had it in his head, so Rabig said, that he could pick up nuggets at the Lion Head."

"The Lion Head?" repeated Dick. "Where is that?"

"It's a good distance from here, Dick, I can tell ye that. It's to the northwest o' the Klondyke. A wild place. It's called the Lion Head acause thar's a mountain thar thet looks like a lion's head. I was thar onct, prospectin' around. But I didn't find any gold thar. But some have found gold," added the old miner.

"How will Tom get there?" questioned Sam.

"Thet's the strangest part o' it," resumed Jack Wumble. "It appears as how he fell in with a miner named Furner—Ike Furner. Rabig says Furner is a bit touched here." Wumble tapped his forehead. "Well, the two made up their minds to go to Lion Head. Furner told Tom he was sure they could pick up nuggets, if only they could hit the right spot. Furner had some kind o' an outfit an' he got Tom to buy some more things, and away they started. Rabig thought they was both crazy."

"And so they must be!" murmured Dick. "Poor Tom! I hope we catch him before he gets too far into the mountains."

"Did this man Rabig say what name Tom was traveling under?" asked Sam.

"Yes. A mighty queer name, too, Brill Thomas. How do ye account fer that?"

"Brill Thomas!" repeated Dick. "Oh, that's easy. Brill is the name of the college he attends and Thomas is his first name in full. He is out of his mind, but he still retains snatches of names and things, I suppose, and that's how he hit on Brill Thomas for a name."

"He told Rabig he was from the land of Hope—the Valley Brook of Hope," went on Jack Wumble. "Rabig never heard tell o' the location."

"Valley Brook is the farm we live on, and Hope is a school near Brill," said Sam. "Poor, poor Tom! Who would have imagined such a thing as this could happen to him!"

"How far is Lion Head from here?" asked Dick.

"As the crow flies, about five hundred miles."

"Five hundred miles!" exclaimed Sam.

"Yes, an' it's nearly six hundred by the way they'll have to travel," went on Jack Wumble.

This news almost stunned the Rover boys. Was it possible that Tom was undertaking a trip of six hundred miles into the little-known portion of Alaska?

"He'd never do such a thing if he was in his right mind," said Dick. "We must catch him just as soon as we can!"

"That is why I hired passage on this boat," said the old miner. "I'm calkerlatin' we can head him off. Thet is, if the weather stays good."

"It looks like rain and is getting colder."

"Right ye are, Dick. An' when it gits cold up here, it gits cold, I kin tell ye thet. Last winter I 'most froze to death up in my shack," added Jack Wumble.

The trip on the boat to Lindy Falls was without special incident. There were about a dozen passengers, all miners and prospectors, who did not care to wait for any of the regular boats. They were a rather good-natured set, and whiled away the time by swapping stories and arguing about the best way to locate paying claims and getting out the gold.

Lindy Falls was reached one afternoon about two o'clock. It was little more than a boat and trading station and here the Rover boys got their first sight of Alaskan Indians, members of the Chilkoot tribe.

Immediately on landing they made inquiries concerning Tom and the miner named Ike Furner. They soon learned that Furner was a well-known character, and from a trader heard that this man and his young companion had set off but a few hours before.

"I think they went to Dawson City," said a man standing nearby. "Anyway, Furner told me he was goin' there first, an' then up to Lion Head."

This put a new view on the matter, and the boys and Jack Wumble questioned the stranger. The upshot was that they decided to go directly to Dawson, that mecca of all gold hunters in Alaska.

"Now, the thing of it is, How can we get to Dawson from here?" said Sam.

"That's easy," replied Jack Wumble. "Just leave it to me."

Inside of an hour their arrangements were made and they were off. Previous to going they made more inquiries concerning Tom and his strange companion, and reached the conclusion that the pair had really headed for Dawson.

"But there is no telling how soon they will change their minds and go somewhere else," said Dick, with a sigh.

It is not my purpose to tell the particulars of the tedious journey to Dawson City, about three hundred and fifty miles north of Skagway. At that time all of the improvements that now exist had not been made and the crowd suffered from many inconveniences.

But the boys were surprised when they reached Dawson to find it so "up to date," as Sam expressed it. They had expected to see a rough mining town—and that is what Dawson was but a handful of years ago. Instead, they say a built-up city, with many stores and not a few hotels.

"Goin' to be a reg'lar 'Frisco some day," said Jack Wumble. "Beats all how the towns grow up here!"

The party had arrived in Dawson late at night and put up at the best hotel to be found. Immediately after breakfast the search for Tom was renewed.

It had rained the day before and now it was

blustery and cold, with a suggestion of snow in the air. The boys were glad enough to don their sweaters under their coats.

"Ye'll have to git some heavy clothin' if ye go North," said the old miner.

"I hope Tom is dressed warm enough," said Sam. "It would be too bad if he took sick, along with his other troubles."

For two days the boys and the old miner hunted around Dawson for some trace of the missing one. They visited all sorts of places, but all to no purpose. During that time the weather grew suddenly colder and on the second night came a light fall of snow.

"Won't be long now before winter will be on us," announced Jack Wumble. "And winter up here is somethin' wuth rememberin', believe me!"

The next morning found Dick at a large trading store, where many miners and prospectors purchased their supplies. Here he asked all newcomers if they had seen or heard of Tom or Ike Furner.

"Sure, I see Furner!" cried one old prospector. "See him yesterday afternoon."

"Where?" demanded Dick, eagerly.

"Over on the Lion Head trail."

"Alone?"

"No, he had a young feller with him."

CHAPTER XX

IN THE MOUNTAINS OF ALASKA

"SAM, I think we are in for a heavy snow to-day."

"I think so myself, Dick. How much further do we go?"

"About two miles," came from Jack Wumble. "I reckon I got a bit off the trail yesterday, but I know I am right now, boys."

"But where is Tom?" came from Sam.

"He must be right ahead of us—if what we have been told is true," answered his brother.

The conversation recorded above took place just ten days after Dick and Sam arrived in Dawson City. During that time the Rover boys and Jack Wumble had spent two days in buying the necessary outfit, to follow Tom and his strange companion to the wild region in Alaska known as Lion Head. The start had been made, and now the three found themselves on a narrow mountain trail in a country that looked to be utterly uninhabited.

For three days they had been close behind Tom and Ike Furner, this being proven by the remains of campfires and other indications. Once they had met some prospectors returning to the Klondyke and these men had told of passing the pair ahead, and that Furner had said they were bound for a spot not many miles from Lion Head called Twin Rocks.

"I never heard o' Twin Rocks before," said Jack Wumble. "But if it is nigh Lion Head we ought to be able to locate it."

"Provided we don't get snowed in before we reach it," returned Sam.

On and on trudged the three. They had left the last supply depot behind. They had passed only a handful of white folks and a band of five Indians.

"Do you know, I didn't like the looks of those Indians we passed yesterday," remarked Dick, as they went forward over the rough, upward trail.

"They looked pretty sharply at our outfits," said Sam. "I guess they'll like to own them," he added.

"We have got to keep our eyes open," said Jack Wumble. "Them Injuns ain't above stealin' if they git a chanct."

"In such an out-of-the-way place as this, we

can't afford to lose our things," asserted Dick.

"Maybe we had better set a guard, at night," suggested his brother.

"Oh, we don't want to lose any sleep, if we don't have to."

It had grown colder and colder, and now the wind swept around them in anything but a pleasant fashion. About noon came a flurry of snow.

"I don't like that," said Dick, shaking his head and looking up at the darkening sky.

"Oh, let's hope it won't amount to much, Dick," replied Sam.

The traveling was steadily upward, for they had to pass over a high hill to get into the valley leading to Lion Head. There was something of a trail, made by wild animals originally and now used by prospectors. This wound in and out among the rock and bushes. The footing was uncertain, and more than once one or another would go down in a hole.

"Talk about walking!" gasped Sam, after pulling himself out of a hole well concealed by bushes. "I'm thankful I didn't break a leg that time."

"An' ye can be thankful ye didn't stir up no snakes," came from Jack Wumble.

"Are there snakes up here, Jack?"

"So they say—although I never see none."

"It's pretty cold for snakes," remarked Dick. "They only come out in the summer time."

"I wish we were on horseback," said Sam, with a sigh.

"Hosses would be fine, if we could feed 'em," answered Jack Wumble. "But ye can't do thet when the ground is covered with snow."

"The outfits are so heavy, Jack."

"True, my boy, but thet can't be helped. We'll be lucky if our grub holds out."

It was after four o'clock when they reached the top of the hill. Had it been clear they might have seen for many miles around them, but now the dullness in the sky hid what was in the distance from view.

"Lion Head is over thar," said Jack Wumble, pointing with his hand. "An' Twin Rocks can't be far off."

"And how far is Lion Head from here?" questioned Sam.

"Betwixt twenty an' thirty miles, Sam."

"Then maybe we'll reach there by to-morrow night."

"Let us hope so, lad. O' course you must remember we've got the wust part o' this journey to go."

"Perhaps we'll catch Tom before we get to Lion Head," suggested Dick.

"Not by the way he has been traveling," answered his brother. "It does beat the nation how he and that Furner have been able to get over the ground."

On the top of the hill the wind was blowing a regular gale and the boys and the old miner were glad enough to go down on the other side, where they would be somewhat sheltered. But even below it was cold, and the air seemed to strike to their very backbones.

"Winter is comin' all right enough," announced Jack Wumble. "We'll be lucky if we git out o' here afore it catches us."

They trudged along until all were too weary to walk another step. They were keeping their eyes open for a spot where they might camp for the night, when Dick uttered a cry.

"Look! They must have remained here last night!"

The others gazed to where he pointed and saw, in a shelter of the rocks, the remains of a campfire. Beside the ashes lay a part of a broken strap and also some fine shavings from a stick.

"Ike Furner's mark," remarked Wumble, pointing to the shavings. They had been told by several men that one of Furner's habits was to whittle a stick. He never rested and talked but what he got out his jackknife and started to cut on a bit of wood. At another campfire, two days back, they had come across a heap of just such whittlings.

"How new is that campfire?" asked Dick, of the old miner.

Jack Wumble examined the heap of dead ashes with care.

"I should say not more'n a day—maybe not thet," he answered. "Boys, I reckon we're close on 'em."

"Oh, if only it wasn't so dark and we weren't so tired!" murmured Sam.

"We can't do much in the darkness, and with a storm coming on," returned Dick. "We'll have to wait until morning. But we had better start out directly it is daylight."

While the others were preparing supper, Dick commenced to arrange the shelter for the night. While he was doing this he noticed something white fluttering on the ground in the wind. He picked it up. It was a sheet of paper, evidently a page torn from a notebook.

"Look what I found," he said, coming close to the light of the campfire. He gazed at the sheet with deep interest. "Well, I never! Sam, look at this!" he cried.

"What is it, Dick?"

"I think Tom wrote this. Poor fellow! Isn't it too bad!"

The sheet of paper had been scribbled on with a lead pencil. The writing was in all sorts of curves, and was largely as follows:

To To To To Ro Ro Ro To
Ro To Bri To Ro Bri
Nel Nel Nel Di S S
To Ro To Ro Tover Tomer
Nel Nel Nel Nel Neltom

"Oh, Dick, what do you make of this?"

"What do I make of it? Can't you see, Sam? Tom was trying to think. He wanted to get something that was hidden away in his memory —his own name, and mine and yours, and Nellie's, and the name of Brill. Maybe a flash of his real self came back to him."

"Oh, if it only would, Dick! Yes, you must be right. First he tried his best to write Tom Rover, but all he got was To Ro, and then he went to Bri for Brill and Nel for Nellie, and Di and S for Dick and Sam. It's as plain as day. It's just like a little child trying to write."

"And it's enough to make a fellow cry," was the sober response.

The two boys studied the paper for a long

time and let Jack Wumble look at it. Then, somewhat silently, all sat down to supper. Their hard walk had made them hungry and they ate every scrap of what had been prepared.

By the time they were ready to turn in, it had begun to snow. The had found a shelter under a cliff of rocks, with some brushwood to keep off the most of the wind. They rolled themselves in their blankets and soon all were in the land of dreams.

Dick had slumbered the best part of several hours, when he suddenly awoke with a start. Some furry body had swept across his face. He sat up in bewilderment and looked around the camp, lit up only by the flickering rays of the dying fire. Then he gave a gasp. From beyond the dying fire two savage eyes were gazing at him intently. Without hesitation he reached down under his blanket, brought out the pistol he carried, and fired.

CHAPTER XXI

AT THE FOOT OF THE CLIFF

CRACK!

The report of the pistol in that confined space sounded loud and clear, and brought Sam and Jack Wumble to their feet with a bound.

"What's the matter, Dick?"

"What ye firing at?"

"Some wild animal. It just leaped over me!" cried the one who had used the firearm. Dick was now on his feet, too, and all stepped away from the shelter of the cliff.

Following the discharge of the weapon had come a short sharp bark or yelp, showing that the animal had been hit. Now followed more barks and yelps from a distance.

"A fox—an Alaskan fox, thet's wot it was," said Jack Wumble. "An' I reckon as how ye hit him, Dick."

"I'm sure I did, for I aimed right at him, and he wasn't over twenty feet away," was the reply. "Wonder if he'll come back?"

"I don't think so—not if he's hurted," returned the old miner. "He must have been putty hungry to come so clost. Must have smelt our grub."

"Maybe he wasn't alone," suggested Sam. "I'd hate to have a pack of foxes come down on me."

"I don't think you'll find any pack around here," answered Jack Wumble. "They ain't so plentiful. But I'll tell ye what we might run across, an Alaskan moose—an' they ain't no nice beast to meet at close quarters."

Some extra brushwood had been gathered before retiring and now a portion of it was heaped on the fire, so that they might have more light. The barking and yelping had died away in the distance, and all around the camp it was as silent as a tomb.

"It's snowing yet," remarked Sam, as he went out to look at the sky. "But it doesn't seem to be very heavy."

"If only we're not snowed in until after we find Tom!" murmured his brother.

Gradually the excitement died away and then they laid down to rest once more. But Dick was nervous and only got into a doze, and he was glad when morning came.

The sky was now dull and heavy, "jest filled

with snow," as Jack Wumble expressed it. The soft flakes were still coming down, but no thicker than they had fallen during the night. The ground was covered with white to a depth of two inches. There was a gentle wind from the northwest.

"Let us not lose any more time than we can help," said Sam. "In such weather as this, every minute may count."

"Right ye are," responded the old miner. "We'll have breakfast quick as we kin an' be off."

Traveling that morning was comparatively easy and they covered quite a number of miles. But then they commenced to climb the mountain leading to Lion Head and Twin Rocks and progress became more difficult.

"Some work, eh, Sam?" remarked Dick, after they had helped each other over some slippery rocks on the trail.

"Do you think Tom and his companion got over these, Dick?"

"I suppose they did. It's the only thing that looks like a trail around here. If they didn't stick to this they'd soon become lost. And being lost on a mountain isn't very nice—you know that."

The snow was still coming down, and to the

boys it seemed heavier than before. Jack Wumble looked at the sky many times and shook his head slowly.

"We'll be in fer it by to-morrow," he said. "An' then nobuddy can tell how long it will keep up. Winter is comin' sure!"

"Then the sooner we find Tom and get back to Dawson with him the better."

It was about five o'clock in the afternoon when they reached a spot where the trail ran along the bottom of a tall cliff. Far below them was the valley they had crossed in the morning, now all but shut out from their view by the falling snow.

"Don't either of ye slip here," cautioned Jack Wumble. "Because, if ye do, thar ain't no tellin' whar ye'll fetch up."

"I'll be as careful as possible," answered Dick.

"And so will I," added Sam.

The old miner was in the lead, with Sam coming next, and Dick bringing up the rear. Thus nearly half a mile more was slowly covered.

"We ought to be drawing close to Tom now," said Dick.

"I've got an idea!" cried his brother. "Why didn't we think of it before? Let us call to him, and fire one of the pistols."

"All right," said the old miner. "'Twon't do no harm."

All three raised their voices in a lusty shout, and Dick fired a shot into the air. Then they listened intently. There was no answer of any kind.

"Let us try it again," suggested Sam. "Now then, all together!"

This time their yell was thrice repeated, and Dick fired two shots. They waited several seconds for an answer.

"Listen!" exclaimed Dick. "I hear something!"

All strained their ears, and from a great distance made out an answering cry. It appeared to come from somewhere above them.

"I believe Tom and that man with him are on the trail above the cliff!" cried Dick.

"Just what I think," answered his brother. "Oh, if only we could climb right up there, instead of going away around!"

"Ain't no way as I can see to do it," said Jack Wumble, looking at the bare wall of rocks. "We'll have ter go on till we reach some sort o' a break."

Once again they cried out and again came the answering call. But those above them were so far away that it was impossible to make out what was said.

"I've got it!" cried Dick. "If that is Tom I'll give him a call he'll know."

"The old Putnam Hall locomotive whistle?" queried Sam.

"Yes. Now then, both together, Sam, and as loud and distinct as possible."

Both youths took a deep breath, and then out on the snowy air rang a sharp, shrill whistle, once, twice, three times, rising and falling in a fashion known only to the cadets of the military school.

"By gosh, thet's some whistle!" remarked Jack Wumble, in admiration.

Again all three listened intently. There was a long spell of silence, and then from a distance came an answering whistle, that sounded like an echo of their own.

"It's Tom!" screamed Sam and clapped his hands.

"Yes, it must be. Nobody else could imitate that whistle so perfectly," returned his brother.

"Oh, let us go on! We must get to him," went on Sam, impatiently. "Maybe that whistle will bring him to his right senses, Dick!"

"I'm afraid that is too much to expect, Sam. But I am glad he remembered the whistle, anyway. It shows that he hasn't forgotten everything."

"Let us yell that we are coming, and for them to wait," suggested the old miner.

"That's it," answered Dick. "Now then, I'll lead off."

And loud and clear rang the cry:

"We are coming! We are coming! Wait for us! Wait! Wait!"

To this some answer came back, but what it was they could not make out. Then, in the silence that followed, they picked up their traps once more and went forward on the wearisome trail.

With each yard of advance the walking became more difficult. In some spots the rocks were covered with snow and they had to proceed with caution, for fear of a nasty tumble. They were climbing upward steadily and they noted with satisfaction that the cliffs seemed to become correspondingly lower.

"We'll be up there in quarter of an hour more," said Jack Wumble. "But don't ye try to go too fast. This trail is gittin' wuss an' wuss."

At last they came to some rocks where further progress seemed impossible. There had been something of a landslide, and big rocks covered the footpath for a distance of a hundred feet or more.

They gazed around the spot in perplexity.

"Well, one thing is certain," said Sam. "Tom and that man must have come this way. If they could get over these rocks we ought to be able to do the same thing."

"I think I see a way," said Dick. "Yes, here are some footprints in the snow and on this fallen tree. They climbed up by holding on to those branches. We can do the same thing."

"Don't ye try it!" yelled Jack Wumble. "Thet tree is loose! It might carry ye to the bottom of the mountain!"

"Hark!" called out Sam. "I hear something! What is that?"

All listened. From a distance came a curious swishing and cracking sound, followed by a wild sort of yell. Then came a crash—and then—utter silence.

CHAPTER XXII

IKE FURNER'S CAMP

"Dick, what was that?"

"I'm sure I don't know, Sam. Sounded like something falling."

"It was a tree sliding down the mountain," put in Jack Wumble. "A tree jest like the one you was goin' to take hold on."

"And somebody on it!" gasped Sam. "Oh, do you suppose it was Tom?"

At this question the old miner shrugged his shoulders.

"Ain't no tellin', Sam. Let us hope not, fer if he went down the mountain side——"

"He'd be killed!" finished Dick, and shuddered.

They listened and called out. But no answer came back, and they heard nothing more but the humming of the wind through the trees, for it had begun to blow stronger than before.

"Let's go a little further than this trail," suggested Jack Wumble. "It looks to be better walking yonder."

"But we don't want to lose our way," returned Sam, rather impatiently. The strange happenings of the day were getting on his nerves.

"We can come back here, if we need to," was the old miner's reply.

The Rovers followed him through some brushwood and then up a rough incline. Here the bushes growing between the rocks aided them, although they had to put on gloves, to keep from getting their hands badly scratched, for some of the growth was thorny.

"Well, here we are at last!" cried Sam, when the upper level of the trail was gained. He was almost out of breath, for the climb had been a long and hard one.

They were now in the midst of a field, with the snow coming down thickly all around them. Wumble led the way, looking for the spot above the fallen tree. To one side was the mountain top, to the other the valley, but all cut off from their view by the falling flakes of snow. It was so dark that they could scarcely distinguish the trail, even though Wumble was sure they were on it.

"Why not light a torch?" suggested Dick. "That will help us, and may make the others see us—if they are near by."

This was considered a good suggestion, and the old miner picked out an extra dry bush that was long and slender. The top ignited readily, and he quickly swung it into a blaze. Then they went on once more, holding the torch at arm's length.

It was well that the light had been made, as they speedily found out. Scarcely had they gone a hundred yards further when they reached a split in the mountain side.

"Stop!" yelled the old miner, and came to a halt at the very brink of a crevice ten or twelve feet wide and of unknown depth.

"There's a tree bridge!" said Dick, as the torch was swung around to light up the vicinity.

He pointed to where a slender tree had been cut down and allowed to fall across the chasm. It made a fairly good bridge, although they had to cross with care and only one at a time. Their traps they threw over the opening.

With the snow now blowing directly in their faces, they marched forward once more, Wumble throwing the light as far ahead as possible. Soon they reached another climb, up a series of rocks that looked almost like a pair of stairs.

"Look!" cried the old miner, a few minutes later, and he stopped to pick something up out of the snow. It was a wooden pipe.

"It must be that Ike Furner's," said Dick. "Tom doesn't smoke."

"Why, look, the pipe has tobacco in it, and it's still lit!" exclaimed Sam. "It couldn't have been dropped very long ago!"

"And that proves that the owner must be close by!" put in his brother. "Let's call!" And he set up a ringing shout, in which Sam and Jack Wumble joined.

For fully a minute no answer came back. Then, from some height above them, issued an answering cry.

"Wave the torch, Jack!" exclaimed Dick, and the old miner did as requested.

All strained their eyes.

"I see a light!" exclaimed Sam. "See, over yonder!"

"I see it," came from the others.

Forward they went, in the direction of the light, which flickered uncertainly through the falling snow. They had to climb around many rocks and bushes, and occasionally they lost sight of the beacon ahead. But at last, mounting another rise, they came in full view of a campfire, located at the entrance to a cave-like opening in the side of the mountain.

A man was standing close to the campfire, a tall, thin individual, with a shock of hair and a heavy beard. He was dressed in a typical miner's costume and in his hands was a pistol.

"Who goes there?" he cried, in a high-pitched, nervous voice. "Don't come any closer until I know who you are," and he raised his pistol and pointed it at those who approached.

"Don't shoot, stranger," called out Jack Wumble, as he and the Rovers came to a halt. "Are you Ike Furner?" he went on.

"I am. Who are you?"

"I'm a miner from Black Run. My handle is Jack Wumble. These are two friends o' mine, Dick an' Sam Rover. We ain't goin' to harm you. We are lookin' fer a young feller thet's lost, that's all."

"We are looking for my brother," added Dick. "His name is Tom Rover. I think he was traveling with you." They had now come close enough to see that Ike Furner was alone.

"Don't know no Tom Rover," was the slow response. "There's a young feller with me, but his name is Brill Thomas."

"And where is he now?" asked Sam, impatiently.

"Was you below here a while ago, shoutin'?" asked Ike Furner, without answering the last question.

"Yes."

"Well, he went off to meet you."

"To meet us!" exclaimed Dick. "Which way did he go?"

"Same way you came."

"But we didn't meet him," cried Sam and Dick, in a breath.

"I dunno nuthin' about that, stranger. When my partner heard you a-callin' an' heard that queer whistle you gave he got all excited, an' said he must see who it was. I told him he'd better wait till you came along, but he wouldn't do it—said he couldn't—that he had remembered somethin' an' he was afraid he was goin' to forgit it ag'in."

"Poor Tom! That whistle must have made him remember who he was!" said Sam. He turned to his brother. "Where can he be now? Oh, Dick, do you remember that strange noise——"

"Yes! yes! If he had a tumble——" Dick could not finish.

"We'd better search into this," came promptly from Jack Wumble. He held out the pipe he had picked up. "Is this yours?" he asked, of the other man.

"It sure is!" cried Ike Furner, his eyes lighting up with pleasure. "I thought sure she was gone fer good. I suppose ye found her on the trail."

"I did."

"Thanks," and the other miner put the precious pipe in his pocket. Then he gazed curiously at the crowd before him. "I don't understand this nohow," he muttered. "That feller who was with me was all right till you called an' whistled, then he acted plumb locoed."

"He is our brother," explained Dick, "and he is a bit out of his mind. But we can't waste time explaining just now. We must hunt him up before this storm gets any worse."

"That's the talk," said Sam.

"I don't see why he didn't meet you."

"We are afraid he had a tumble," answered Dick, and told about the strange swishing and crashing they had heard.

"By gum! Maybe he went down into thet split in the rocks!" cried Ike Furner. "I yelled to him to be careful o' thet openin'. But he was in sech a hurry——" The miner did not finish.

"I'll get a fresh torch and we'll go back," said Jack Wumble. His face wore a sober look. "A tumble down thet openin' would be putty bad," he added.

"Want me to go along?" asked Ike Furner.

"You can go if you want to," answered Dick.

"But fix your traps so that no wild animals can get at the food."

"Oh, the grub is safe enough. I'll keep a good fire burnin'," answered the prospector. They could readily see that he was a peculiar man, but with a kindly heart. Family troubles had caused him to try his fortunes in this out of the way portion of the globe.

It did not take long for them to build up the campfire and get an extra torch. This done, all set off in the direction of the split in the rocks, Jack Wumble leading the way and the others coming in a bunch behind him.

The Rover boys knew not what to say or what to think. Had Tom tumbled into that awful opening, and if so, was he alive or dead?

"If he went down there I don't see how he could escape," whispered Sam to his brother. "Why, when I crossed on that tree I couldn't see the bottom!"

"Let us hope he didn't take that tumble," was the low reply.

CHAPTER XXIII

A SLIDE DOWN THE MOUNTAIN SIDE

"My gracious, Dick! It sure is snowing some now!"

"Yes, and it is getting colder every minute."

"If we don't get out of the mountains putty quick we'll be snowed in," came from Jack Wumble.

"Did you calkerlate to git back to Dawson afore winter sot in?" inquired Ike Furner, curiously.

"Why of course!" cried Sam.

"I don't see how you are goin' to make it."

"Oh, we must get back," said Dick. "If only we could find Tom," he added, with a sigh.

It was fully an hour after they had left the campfire at the entrance to the cave of the mountain. They had walked to the chasm where they thought Tom might have had a tumble and crossed and recrossed it several times. But they had found no traces of the missing Rover boy.

"If only we knew whether he went down in

that opening!" said Sam, for at least the tenth time. "Dick, do you suppose we can climb down into it?"

"Not without a rope, Sam. The sides are too steep and slippery."

Time and again they called down. But no answer came back. If Tom was down there he was either unconscious or dead.

And now it had begun to snow harder than ever. The air was so full of the white flakes that they could not see ten feet in any direction. It was a typical Alaskan snowstorm. There was a sweep to the wind that found the very marrow of their bones.

What to do next the Rovers did not know, nor could the two miners suggest anything. Finally, however, Ike Furner mentioned something that set the youths to thinking.

"See here!" he cried. "The old tree is gone!"

"What tree?" asked all three of the others.

"Why, the big hemlock as was hangin' over the cliff. She was a whopper, I kin tell you—biggest tree in these parts."

"Where was that tree?" asked Dick.

"Right here, whar you see the holes. The snow has covered the spot putty well, but I know the tree was here when we come up."

"It must have been that tree we heard sliding down the mountain side," exclaimed Dick. "Maybe Tom didn't go down into the chasm at all, but slid down the mountain on the tree!"

"That's so!" put in Sam, eagerly. "And he may not be hurt!"

"Well, a slide like thet wouldn't be anything to sneeze at," remarked Jack Wumble. "Especially if the tree took to rollin' over an' over!"

"I'm goin' to investigate," said Dick, and commenced to crawl out on the edge of the cliff.

"You be careful!" roared Wumble. "It's slippery an' dangerous out there!"

"Let us join hands," suggested Sam, and this was done, all forming a chain, to keep Dick from going over the edge of the cliff. He took the torch in one hand, that he might light the way in the darkness and the flying snow.

At last Dick found himself on the very edge of the cliff at the point where the giant tree had stood. To his surprise the cliff was not perpendicular there, but formed a slope leading to another ridge some fifty feet below. What was beneath this was hidden from view by the falling snow.

"I think I can crawl down there," he said to the others. "Anyway, I am going to try it."

"Wait! I've got a lariat in my pack," said

Ike Furner. "I'll git that. It will be better'n nuthin'." And off he sped for the article mentioned.

When he came back Dick tied one end of the lariat around his waist, and while the others held fast he crawled down the slope. He had to keep on his hands and knees, and once he slipped a distance of several yards, the others stopping him with a jerk.

"Be careful—the lariat might snap!" sang out Sam.

"It's better walking down here," answered Dick. "I think——"

He did not finish, for just then his body swung down into a hollow, filled with snow and with some dripping water that had commenced to freeze. There was a snap, and the end of the lariat came back in the faces of those above.

"There he goes!" yelled Jack Wumble, and pointed down to where the torch could be seen whirling around and around. Soon it was hidden from view by the snow.

"Dick! Dick!" yelled Sam. "Are you safe?"

A yell came back, but what was said those above could not make out. Sam's face went white, and he looked inquiringly at Jack Wumble.

"Where do you suppose he went to?" asked Ike Furner.

Wumble shook his head.

"Don't know, unless he slid clar down to the valley," he returned. "This is certainly the wust yet."

"I'm going down after him," said Sam, bravely.

"Be careful, lad, it may cost ye your life."

"I don't care—I'm going to find Dick—and Tom, too."

The youngest Rover was just worked up enough to be reckless. And when Sam got that way nothing could hold him back.

"I'm going back, to get something to eat for all hands—in case we need it," he said. "Then I'll crawl down somehow and learn the truth. If Tom and Dick are all right, I'll fire one shot from my pistol. Then you'll know we are coming up as soon as possible. If I fire two shots you'll know we are all right, but we can't come up right away. If I fire three shots you'll know I need help. In that case come down, packs and all, and we'll find some kind of a camping spot below."

So it was settled, and having gone back to where the traps had been left, the youngest Rover made up a small bundle for himself, and also procured another torch. The others accompanied him to where Dick had disappeared.

"I hate to see ye leavin' me," said Jack Wumble, with feeling. "Maybe it would be better to wait till mornin', when it was lighter."

"No, Jack, I can't wait—and have Dick down there, and Tom, too. For all we know, both of them may be dying!"

That was all Sam said, and to this the old miner could not reply. Ike Furner looked on, but did not open his mouth. He was waiting to hear the full particulars concerning the young man he had known as Brill Thomas.

Down and down went Sam, the snow soon hiding the two miners from his view. He had to proceed with care, fearing a tumble such as his big brother had taken. Where there was water, ice was forming on the rocks, making the descent more dangerous than ever.

"I don't know how a fellow is to get back that way," he said to himself. "Guess we'll have to walk around by the trail."

It was now intensely cold and the wind was blowing almost a gale. He was glad when he reached something of a hollow, where he could crouch down and regain his breath.

"Dick! Dick!" he cried, many times, but no answer came back. Either his brother was too far away to hear him or was too badly hurt to make reply.

Down and down climbed Sam until he felt he must be approaching the foot of the mountain. He had his torch still in hand, having often carried it in his teeth while holding fast. In some spots the snow was now over a foot deep, and his footing was, consequently, more uncertain than ever.

Suddenly he found himself on the edge of a small cliff, the last on the mountain side. Without knowing it, he had crossed the trail leading upward three times. He stepped on some ice on the rocks, and the next instant was launched into space.

Sam had no time to get scared. Forth into the descending snow he was tossed, and down he went, to land first in a tree and then in some thick bushes growing close by. The wind was knocked completely out of him, and for the moment he could not move.

"Phew! that was a tumble!" he murmured, as he tried to sit up. He was wedged so tightly in the bushes that he could scarcely move. It was far from a pleasant situation, yet he realized that coming down first on the tree and then in the bushes had saved him from broken bones if not from death. He was considerably scratched up, but just then paid no attention to the hurts.

At last he managed to crawl out on the ground, or rather the snow, which was deeper in the valley than it had been up on the mountain. His torch had been extinguished, so all was dark around him.

"Dick!" he called, as loudly as he could. "Dick, are you anywhere around?"

"Sam!" came the faint reply. "Is that you? Yes, I am over here. Help me. I am wedged in between the trees and can't move!"

"Is Tom down here too?"

"I don't know."

CHAPTER XXIV

IN WHICH TOM IS FOUND

GUIDED by his brother's voice Sam at last found Dick. As the latter had said, he was wedged between two tall trees and in anything but a comfortable position. And how to release him was a problem.

"I guess I had better climb up and bend one of the trees over by my weight," suggested Sam. "I don't see any other way."

"All right, Sam. Only be careful and don't fall and let the tree snap back on me," answered Dick, weakly. In his cramped position he could scarcely breathe.

With great care Sam ascended the slimmest of the two trees, pushing it as far away from the other as possible. As he went up his weight told, and presently the tree commenced to bend down, away from the other.

"That's better—now I can move a little," cried Dick. "Go on! There, that's enough. All right, Sam, you can come down." And then

Dick scrambled out in the snow and his brother joined him.

"Did you see anything at all of Tom?" asked the youngest Rover, as soon as both could get their breath.

"Not a thing, Sam. But I saw the tree that fell—it's caught on the cliff above here."

"Yes, I saw that—just before I took a tumble."

"Then you fell too?"

"Only from the last cliff. I landed in a tree and then some bushes, and got pretty well scratched. But come on, if you're able, and we'll look for Tom."

"What's that bundle you have strapped to your back?"

"I brought a little food along, in case we had to stay down here until to-morrow."

"I see. Wait, we'll light a torch first—we can't do much in the dark."

Dry brushwood was to be had in plenty, and the boys not only lit torches, but also made a fire, to light up the scene all around them Then they set off on their hunt, going up and down the base of the cliff for several hundred feet. It was now snowing so furiously that progress was difficult.

"We'll be snowed in, that's certain," remarked

Sam, as they moved about, swinging their torches to the right and left.

"I don't care—if only we find Tom, and he isn't seriously hurt," returned his brother.

"But it's no fool of a thing, to be snow-bound in Alaska, Dick! I've heard of miners being starved to death—not being able to get any-where for food!"

"Yes, I've heard of that, too. But do you want to give up this hunt for Tom?"

"Indeed not! I'll stick it out no matter what comes!" answered Sam, quickly.

As they moved along Dick presently saw what he thought was a rock or mound of dirt in front of him, covered with snow. He was about to step over it, when something prompted him to scrape at the object with his foot. The next in-stant he let out a cry.

"It's Tom!"

"Are you sure?" gasped Sam, who was a few yards away.

"Yes! yes! Here, hold my torch," went on Dick, and as Sam took the light, Dick knelt in the snow and raised up the inanimate form. It was Tom, true enough, with an ugly cut on his forehead, from which the blood had been flow-ing.

"Is—is he de—dead?" asked Sam, hoarsely.

"HERE, HOLD MY TORCH," SAID DICK.

The Rover Boys in Alaska. *Page* 226

"I—I don't know, Sam," was the slow answer. "You lead the way and I'll carry him back to where we built that fire."

"Oh, Dick, can't you tell if he is breathing?"

Dick put his ear to Tom's breast and for a moment there was a painful silence.

"I think he is breathing, Sam, but I am not quite sure. We'll get to the fire, and give him something hot to drink."

Sam led the way through the snow, carrying both torches, and Dick came after him, with the inanimate form of poor Tom over his shoulder. In a few minutes they reached the fire they had made, and Sam piled on some additional brushwood. Sam had rolled the food and other things he had brought along in a blanket, and this covering was now placed on the snow and Tom was laid on it, partly under the shelter of some bushes.

The two brothers got down and worked over the unconscious one for over a quarter of an hour. They had a bottle of a stimulent the doctor had given them for Tom, and now they forced a dose of this down the lad's throat. Then they rubbed his hands and wrists. Gradually they saw a change in Tom. He began to breath a little deeper and muttered something in an undertone.

"Tom! Tom!" cried Dick. "Don't you know me? Tom! It's Dick and Sam! Wake up, old man, that's a good fellow!"

"Oh, my head! Oh, my head!" came, with a groan, and the sufferer slowly stretched himself. Then he put one hand up to his forehead. "Oh, dear, what a crack I got!"

"Never mind, Tom, you'll soon be yourself," cried Sam, a big relief showing itself in his voice. Tom wasn't dead, perhaps after all he wasn't seriously hurt.

"Oh, my head!" was all the answer Tom made just then. He opened his eyes for an instant and then closed them again.

"Wonder if he will know us?" whispered Sam to Dick.

"I hope so," was the answer. "But come, we must do all we can for him. I don't think we can move him very far. But we'd be better off if we were in the shelter of that cliff."

"Wait, I'll hunt up a spot, Dick. But hadn't I better fire a shot first?" And Sam told of the signals that had been arranged.

"Yes, give 'em two shots," said the big brother. "If we want help later we can fire some more." And the shots were discharged without further delay.

This done, a shelter close to the cliff was selected. Here they cut down some brushwood with a hatchet Sam had brought along, and formed a barrier to keep out the wind and snow. Then another campfire was built and Tom was brought over and placed on the blanket, in a warm and cozy corner.

"Oh, my head!" he muttered, over and over again. Of a sudden he sat up as if in bewilderment. "Where am I?" he cried. "Is it time to get up? Say, Sam, I wonder if I've got time to write that theme I didn't do last night. Songbird said he would give me a few pointers, but I reckon he forgot all about it. Say, what makes it so cold in this room? It's time old Muggs turned on the steam heat."

"Tom! Tom!" said Sam. "Do you know me? Don't you know where you are?"

"Don't I know you? What are you talking about, Sam. Of course I know you. And Dick! Say, how did you get back to college, Dick? And why in thunder——? Well, I declare!" Tom sat up and stared at the campfire and the snow. "How in the name of Washington's sword did I get here?" he gasped.

"Never mind that now, Tom," answered Dick, taking him by the hand. "How do you feel? You had a bad tumble, if you'll remember."

"Tumble? Where did I tumble from? Oh,

I remember—that moving picture show! Say, that Alaskan scene was great, wasn't it? I thought I'd like to go to Alaska after some of those nuggets. Funny, wasn't it?" And poor Tom grinned broadly. "But how did I get here, in the snow and cold. Say, have I been sick again, Dick?" And now the sufferer looked sharply at his brothers.

"Yes, Tom, you've been—very sick," answered Dick, slowly. "How do you feel now? You had a bad tumble, and we were afraid you had been killed."

"Where did I tumble from, the roof of the dormitory?"

"No, you fell down the mountain side."

"Eh? What mountain side?"

"The one right back of you. But don't bother about that now. Just take it easy and rest yourself," went on Dick, soothingly.

"Are you sure no bones are broken?" asked Sam, anxiously.

"I don't remember anything about a tumble," said Tom, slowly. I—I—thought I was in our room at Brill, old number twenty-five. And it wasn't winter either. Say, I can't understand all this. Are we out in the woods back of Brill? Hadn't we better get back? See how it's snowing."

"We won't go back to-night, Tom," answered Dick. "You just take my advice and lie down and keep quiet. If you are hungry you can have something to eat."

"I don't want anything to eat—I had a bang-up supper, the last I can remember. But I seem to be in a fog. I don't remember anything about how I got here. And my head hurts to beat the band! Feels as if a lot of boiler makers were working inside of it!" Tom put his hand up as of old. "I guess I'll—I'll have to—to leave it all to you!" he went on faintly, and then fell back on the blanket, completely exhausted.

CHAPTER XXV

THE SHELTER UNDER THE CLIFF

DESPITE the fact that they were caught in a furious snowstorm, and that there was no telling how long the downfall would last, Sam and Dick felt very happy as they crouched by the camp-fire in the shelter of the cliff. They had found their brother, and he did not seem to be seriously hurt by the long tumble he had taken.

"I guess we had better let him rest quietly, Sam," whispered Dick, as both bent over the sufferer. "It will probably do him more good than anything."

"Just what I think, Dick. But tell me, do you think he is in his right mind now?"

"I can't tell, exactly. One thing is sure, he doesn't seem to remember anything of his trip to this out-of-the-way spot."

"Isn't it queer! I never thought a fellow's mind could play him such tricks!"

"Oh, men have been known to wander away and then come to themselves and not remember a thing about how it happened. Maybe that tumble did him good."

The two boys stirred around the shelter, fixing the fire and making the barrier of brushwood more secure. Tom continued to rest, occasionally muttering to himself.

"We might as well have something to eat, since you brought something along," remarked Dick, presently. "And then we'll have to turn in. We can take turns at sleeping and at watching Tom."

"Do you think we'll be completely snowed in by morning?"

"Let us hope not."

An hour later Sam was sleeping, while Dick sat on some brushwood, tending the fire and keeping an eye on Tom. It was very quiet, and the snow was coming down as thickly as ever. Dick had much to occupy his mind—the perils of the present situation, his father's business affairs, and Dora.

"Poor Dora!" he murmured. "She'll be much worried until she hears from me again. Well, I won't mind all this, if only Tom comes out of it in his right mind." It made Dick sick from head to foot to think that fun-loving Tom might have to go to an asylum. Such a happening would wreck the happiness of every member of the family, and wreck dear Nellie's happiness, too.

Dick remained on watch for three hours and then roused Sam and turned in himself. So the long night passed, Tom continuing to sleep, and only rousing up once and demanding a drink. And he went on sleeping when Dick and Sam arose to get breakfast and form their plans for the day.

It had stopped snowing, but the sky was still overcast. It was colder than before—a drop in the thermometer which meant but one thing—that the long Alaskan winter had arrived. For months to come everything would be frozen up as hard as a rock.

"I'd give a good deal to be back in Dawson," remarked Dick, while munching a scant breakfast. He and Sam had decided to make the food on hand last as long as possible.

"So would I. But I don't see ourselves getting there in this fall of snow—and with more snow in the air."

"I don't see what we're going to do with Tom, if he can't walk. We can't carry him."

"We can make a drag—a sort of sled, Sam—and haul him on that."

"So we can! How queer I didn't think of it! Why, it will be just the thing!" And the face of the youngest Rover brightened up considerably.

Just what move to make next would depend in a great measure on how Tom felt when he roused up. His brothers watched him anxiously, but made no move to wake him.

It was about ten o'clock in the forenoon when a shout was heard, and, looking through the bushes, the boys beheld Jack Wumble and Ike Furner. Each had a pack on his back.

"Hello!" cried Dick, and ran out to meet them.

"Oh, so there ye are!" exclaimed Jack Wumble. "Thought ye must be somewhere around here. How are ye, all right?" he went on, anxiously.

"Yes. A little scratched up, that's all."

"An' Sam, an' Tom?"

"Sam is a bit scratched up, too. We found Tom and he doesn't seem to have any bones broken. But he is very weak, and we are letting him sleep," and Dick gave some particulars.

"We had some job getting off the mountain," said the old miner, and then he added in a somewhat lower tone. "I've told Furner all about Tom and it's all right."

"I reckoned as how he wasn't just O. K.," said Ike Furner. "But then some folks say I ain't jest all right, when I know I am," and he tossed back his head. He was by no means crazy, only peculiar and headstrong.

"Do you think we can get back to Dawson?" asked Sam, who had come forward after Dick.

"Maybe, lad; but it will be a tough journey in this snow," answered Wumble.

"I'm going to stay here an' look fer gold!" cried Ike Furner, stubbornly. "I've got your brother's part of our outfit here." He passed it over. "There's Lion Head, and over yonder is the Split Rocks. I think I'm about due to find a fortune," and he drew himself up to his full height.

"Well, we are not going to stop you," answered Dick. "All we came after was our brother. But it's a pity to leave you here all alone."

"Oh, I won't mind that. I've often been alone in the mountains. Fact is, I rather like it. When a feller is alone he can do just as he pleases."

"That is true," answered Dick, with a faint smile.

"I know some other miners up here," went on Ike Furner. "I'm going to hit for their camp an' stay there till Spring. How is the brother makin' it?"

"He's sleeping now. I think he will be all right. He doesn't remember anything about his trip up here."

An hour went by and Tom roused up. He looked blankly at Jack Wumble and Ike Furner.

"Don't you know me, Tom?" asked the former. "We had some great times out West, years ago."

"Sure I know you," and the sufferer grinned feebly. "You're Jack Wumble, aren't you?"

"That's me. Put her thar, Tom!" And the old miner took Tom's hand and held it tightly. "Glory to heaven! This is like a touch o' old times, this is!"

Then Ike Furner approached, looking at Tom closely. But the youth did not seem to recognize him.

"Know me, too, don't you?" asked the old prospector.

"I—I can't say that I do," was the slow answer, and Tom appeared much perplexed. "Seems to me I've seen you somewhere, but I can't just place you."

"Well, I'll be switched!" muttered Ike Furner. "Thet's the strangest thing I ever hear tell on." He pulled on his rough beard. "Don't remember me a' tall?"

"No. Who are you?"

"Ike Furner, the man you came to Alaska with."

"Alaska! I never went to Alaska!" cried Tom. He commenced to grow excited. "Dick! Sam! What does this mean?" He tried to struggle to his feet, but found himself too weak to do so.

"Keep quiet, Tom," ordered his elder brother. "It's all right. You've been very sick, that's all, and—well, a bit out of your mind. You'll be all right after a while."

"But that man said I went to Alaska."

"So you did. But it's all right, so just take it easy."

"Alaska! Great hambones! Am I in Alaska now?"

"Yes, if you must know. But do be quiet and rest yourself," went on Dick, soothingly.

"What did I do, run away?"

"We'll talk about it later, Tom. You must rest now," and Dick made the sufferer lie down as before. Then he motioned for Ike Furner to come away.

"It's all right, I'll git out—I wouldn't stay fer a farm!" muttered the old gold hunter. "Your brother is as crazy as they make 'em. I'm glad to get shut o' him. Didn't remember me! I can't believe it!" And a little later he bid the crowd farewell and took his departure, to hunt up the other old prospectors he had mentioned. It may be said here that that was the last the Rovers saw or heard of him for a long time to come.

The day passed slowly, the others doing all they could for poor Tom. The sufferer roused up several times and took what nourishment was given to him. His head had been bound up, so that the cut on his forehead did not show. Evidently he was suffering from exposure and the loss of blood.

"We must get him to Dawson somehow," said Dick. "I guess we had better start to-morrow morning early."

"Just what I think," replied Sam.

"Suits me," responded Jack Wumble. "But it ain't going to be no easy job makin' it, boys," he added, seriously.

CHAPTER XXVI

IN THE GRIP OF THE TORNADO

In the morning all thoughts of moving had to be abandoned. It was snowing furiously and the wind was sweeping around them in a perfect gale.

"We're snowbound," said Jack Wumble, after a look around. "Winter this year has come on putty quick."

It was a dismaying state of affairs and Sam and Dick looked at each other questioningly. What was to be done?

Tom was no better nor was he worse. He lay where they had placed him, close to the fire, and took such nourishment as was given to him. At times he appeared quite rational, but once in a while he asked some question that showed he was not altogether in his right mind.

"We could stay here for some time if it wasn't for one thing," remarked Dick. "We have got to have food."

"Just what I was thinking," returned Sam.

"As it is, we haven't enough to last us for more than a week at the most."

"If there was a river anywhere near I'd try my hand at fishin'," said the old miner. "Ye kin get plenty o' fish in Alaska, even if ye have to fish through a hole in the ice fer 'em."

The cold was so intense that the boys were glad enough to stir around in the snow and wind to keep warm. They cut a big pile of firewood and piled the brushwood thickly around the shelter, taking care, however, to keep it from the campfire.

The day went slowly by. At nightfall the snow stopped coming down, but the wind blew as before and if anything it was colder.

"Nothing but ice from now on," announced Jack Wumble, and he was right, by morning everything was frozen up, "as stiff as a stake," as Sam expressed it. The day before they had caught some water dripping from the rocks, for drinking purposes, now they had to melt the ice over the fire to get the liquid.

But the sun was shining brightly and that raised their spirits.

"Don't you suppose, if we made a drag for Tom, that we could get back to Dawson somehow?" questioned Sam, after all had been outside to look at the sky.

"Well, we kin try it, if ye say so," answered Jack Wumble. "It sure ain't no fun stayin' here, with no more grub showin' itself. If I could only shoot a wildcat fer the meat I'd feel better."

With so much brushwood at hand it was an easy matter to construct a rude sled-like drag for poor Tom. To make it more comfortable they heaped on it some tundra moss which they found growing on one of the wind-swept stretches nearby.

"Where are you going to take me?" demanded the sufferer, when told that they were going to leave the place.

"We are going to take you to a safe shelter, Tom, and then home," answered Dick.

"Home! That sounds good!" murmured Tom. "I'll be glad to get there and rest!" and he gave a long-drawn sigh.

The start was made by ten o'clock, Tom being warmly wrapped in blankets, and all the traps being piled on the drag in front and behind him. A rope had been tied fast in front and on this Wumble and Dick pulled, while Sam had hold of the drag itself, to pull and to steer.

It was still bitter cold and many times on the way those hauling the drag stopped, to make sure that Tom was comfortable and in no danger of getting his nose or his ears frostbitten. Fortunately the route was largely down hill, so pulling the long drag was not such a hardship as it otherwise might have been.

At noon they stopped in a small hollow, sheltered from the wind, and made themselves a hot pot of coffee, and ate a frugal lunch. Tom sat up for a few minutes and the others were glad to see that the journey had done him no harm, either physically or mentally.

By the middle of the afternoon it was snowing again and they had all they could do to keep to the trail. The old miner shook his head dubiously.

"Reckon as how we're up against it," was his comment. "If it gits much wuss we'll have to look fer another shelter, boys."

The wind had let up during the middle of the day, but now it commenced to blow with a suddenness that was alarming. It sent the whirling snow into their faces with pitiless fury and almost blinded them, while they breathed with difficulty.

"Got to git out o' this, an' mighty quick too!" gasped Jack Wumble.

"Which way shall we turn, Jack?" questioned Dick. "I can't see at all."

"I think thar's a woods below—let's strike

fer that, lad. It will mean shelter an' firewood, at least."

They hurried on, pulling the long drag after them. They were in a valley and suddenly they came to a broad patch of ice and Sam went sprawling on his back. His brother helped him to arise, and onward they went once more, but with added caution.

"This must be a lake," said Dick, as, after traveling for some time, they found the ice still under their feet. "Or else a river."

"Can it be safe?" asked Sam. "Why, it wasn't frozen over four days ago!"

"We'll be careful," cried Wumble. "Even if it is hard enough, there may be airholes around."

The situation seemed to grow steadily worse. The wind blew so hard that at times they were fairly carried along by it. The snow cut off the view from all sides, so they could not determine in what direction they were traveling.

"Here's something ahead!" cried Wumble, presently. "A hut—a miner's hut!"

"Let's get inside, just as quickly as we can," returned Sam, his teeth chattering. "I'm mo—most frozen stiff!"

The hut was on a small bank, evidently on the shore of the lake, or river, on which they had been traveling. It was closed up tightly, and a pounding on the door brought no response.

"Nobuddy home, I reckon," said Jack Wumble. "Well, here goes to git in," and he pushed on the door.

It was not locked and swung inward, revealing a single room, about twelve feet square and lit up by one small window. Opposite the door was a fireplace, partly filled with cold ashes. On a shelf and on a rude table rested some cooking utensils, and to one side of the hut was a bunk containing some pine tree boughs and several old blankets.

"Hello!" cried Dick. "Anybody in here?"

There was no answer, and a quick look around convinced them that nobody had been in the place for several days if not weeks. Yet on a shelf in a rude locker were a number of stores—beans, coffee, a side of bacon, and several other things.

"Let us start a fire, first thing, and get thawed out," suggested Sam, and this was done, the boys finding plenty of wood piled up behind the hut. They had already brought Tom in from the drag and placed him in the bunk, and now they closed the door.

"In this awful blow, we'll have to watch that fire carefully," warned Wumble. "Ef we don't, we may burn down the shebang over our heads."

The blaze soon warmed them all up and even Tom said he felt better. The boys looked over the stores in the cabin with interest.

"What about touching these?" said Dick to the old miner. "Have we any right to do it? Of course we'd pay for the things."

"We won't touch 'em unless we have to, Dick. It ain't a question o' pay in sech a spot as this. The owner may be comin' back and dependin' on 'em. A man as wants grub won't part with it fer no amount o' gold. Why, I've seen the time, in camp in winter, when a feller wouldn't sell a quart o' plain beans fer a hundred dollars o' dust!"

"Yes, I know that. All right, we'll leave the things alone." And Dick sighed. How good an old fashion home dinner would have tasted to all of them just then!

The wind continued to howl, occasionally rocking the hut in a fashion that alarmed them. Sam asked the old miner if there was any danger of it being tipped over.

"There is allers danger when the wind gits too high," was the reply.

Presently the sparks commenced to blow out into the room and the wind outside grew wilder and wilder. They stamped out the fire and sat huddled together in the darkness, Tom with the rest, for he was now a little stronger and did not want to remain alone.

And then came a shock as paralyzing as it was appalling. The hut seemed to be lifted into the air and whirled around. Then came a crash, and the structure fell over on the ice and snow of the river, or lake, below. The boys tumbled in a heap, with Jack Wumble on top of them. Before they could get up, all felt themselves moving swiftly along in a wind that was blowing little short of a tornado. All was pitch black around them and to get up, or to do anything, was totally out of the question. Sam started to ask Dick a question, when something hit him on the head, and he fell back unconscious.

CHAPTER XXVII

LOST IN THE FIELDS OF ICE

"WHERE in the world are we, Jack?"

"Don't ask me, Dick! I reckon the wind must 'a' swept us up to the North Pole!"

"Tom, are you all right?"

"Well, I'm here," came back faintly from the suffering one. "What did we do, sail through the air?"

"We sailed through something, Tom—and I guess we went about a mile a minute, too. Where is Sam?"

"I don't know," answered the old miner. "It's so snowy I can't see a thing."

"Sam! Sam!" yelled Dick, with as much force as he could command.

There was no reply. If the youngest Rover was nearby he was in no condition to answer the call.

A full hour had elapsed since that terrific gust of wind had tumbled the hut down on the river, for such the sheet of water proved to be. Then had followed a tornado, or hurricane, or cyclone, the boys and the old miner could not tell which. Hut and occupants had been carried along the stream on the ice with the velocity of an express train. From the river they had been swept out over a lake, and finally had landed in a big bank of snow with a crash that had shattered the hut into fragments.

All had been so shaken up that for some minutes nobody could speak. The old miner was the first to recover and he had stumbled around until he found Dick, who was holding poor Tom in his arms. Both of the brothers had been pretty well pounded, but were otherwise uninjured by their thrilling experience.

It was snowing again, the snow now coming down in regular "chunks" as Dick said. The wind had gone down a little, but was still blowing fiercely. All was dark around the remains of the hut.

"Sam! Sam!" yelled Dick, again and again, and staggered around in the snow, searching for the missing one. Then he landed on the ice of the lake and went flat on his back, and Jack Wumble came after him. As they picked themselves up they heard a faint cry and caught sight of Sam, lying but a few yards away.

"Are ye hurted any, lad?" asked Wumble,

who was first at the youngest Rover's side.

"I—I don't know," gasped Sam. "Some—something struck me on th—the head."

With the assistance of the old miner and Dick he arose to his feet, and all three staggered back to where Tom had been left. The ruins of the hut rested against a snowbank, and, to get out of the wind, they crawled between the logs and the snow.

"This is the worst yet," was Dick's comment. "How are we ever to find our way back to Dawson from here?"

Nobody could answer that question. Just now they had all they could do to keep warm.

"You stay here while I take a little look around," said Jack Wumble, presently. "I may learn somethin' wuth knowin'."

"But don't get lost, Jack," cautioned Dick.

"I'll be careful," was the answer.

The old miner was gone less than ten minutes when he set up a shout.

"What have you found?" asked Dick, quickly.

"Here's a signboard," was the reply. "I reckon as how there's a trail here. It says somethin', but I can't make it out."

"Let's light a torch," suggested Sam, and this was done. They brushed the snow from the signboard and read the following, printed in crude letters:

10 mILes to Sublers sTORes

Below this lettering was a crude drawing of a hand pointing up the lake.

"Subler's Stores!" cried the old miner. "I've heard o' that place. It's quite a depot for supplies. If we could only git thar we'd be all right."

"Let's try it," suggested Dick. "The wind is right down the lake, so it will make traveling that much easier."

They labored hard, in the darkness and wind, to construct a drag out of the ruins of the hut. On this they placed Tom and also such of their scanty traps and provisions as still remained to them.

But once out on the lake, they realized that the task before them was no easy one. Here the wind blew with terrific force, sending them further and further away from the shore which they wanted to skirt. It had stopped snowing and seemed to be growing colder.

"I—I ca—can't stand this!" gasped Sam, after a while. "I'm fr—freezing!"

"So—so am I," answered Dick. "Tom, are you all right?"

"I'm pretty co—cold," was the chattered-out reply.

"We can't make it, I reckon," said the old miner, who was as chilled as any of them. "We'll have to go ashore an' git out of the wind an' build a fire to thaw out by."

But getting ashore was out of the question. When they tried to turn around the fierce wind fairly took their breath away. So they continued to advance, the wind at times carrying them almost off their feet.

"We are on the ice and no mistake!" cried Dick, after a while. "See, the wind has blown the snow completely away."

He was right. All around them was the ice, dark and exceedingly slippery. They seemed to be in the midst of a great field of it.

"I don't know where I am now," said Jack Wumble. "We are lost."

"Lost!" echoed Sam.

"That's the truth of it, Sam," replied Dick. "We are lost right out here on this ice."

"But Subler's Stores?"

"I haven't the least idea in what direction they are."

"But if we follow the wind——?"

"The wind seems to be changing. Just watch it."

Dick was right, the wind was shifting, first in one direction, then in another.

"If we stay out here, we'll be frozen stiff," said Tom. As he could not move around he felt the cold more than did the others.

"Let us follow the wind—it is bound to bring us somewhere, and that is better than staying here," said Dick, finally.

For the want of something better to suggest, the others agreed, and on they went once more, dragging Tom and their few traps and stores behind them.

Thus another hour passed. By this time they were so exhausted they could scarcely stand. They staggered onward until Sam fell. He was so weak the others had to assist him to arise.

"I'm all in!" gasped the youngest Rover. "You go on and save yourselves."

"And leave you?" cried Dick. "Never! Sam, you know me better than that," he added, reproachfully.

"But, Dick, I—I can't walk another step!"

"Then sit on the drag with Tom."

"But you and Wumble——"

"We'll pull ye somehow," said the old miner, grimly. "We ought to be gittin' somewhar soon."

It was now dark once more and snowing again. The wind had gone down a trifle, but it still carried them forward, first in one direction and then another.

Presently the drag hit a series of rocks, covered with ice and snow. Over it went, sending Tom and Sam sprawling. Dick and Wumble also fell, for the way had suddenly grown uneven.

"I think we are near the shore now," said Wumble. "Them rocks wouldn't be likely to be out in the middle o' the lake."

"I think I see something!" cried Dick. "Over yonder."

With caution they advanced, and at last made out a small building, located between a numbei of large rocks. All around the building was snow and ice.

"A light!" cried Jack Wumble. "Somebody is thar! This is the best news yet."

He stumbled through the snow and over the ice and rocks until he reached the door of the cabin. He pounded loudly on the portal.

"Who is there?" demanded a rough voice from within.

"Friends," answered the old miner. "Let us in—we are 'most frozen to death."

"Who are you?" went on the voice from inside the cabin. "Be careful now, I am armed."

Cautiously the door to the cabin was opened

and a very old man appeared. He was armed with a shotgun, which he pointed at those outside.

"I can't see ye," he said, slowly. "Come a bit closer, but not too clost, until I make sure who ye are."

"Why, it's Tony Bings!" fairly shouted Jack Wumble. "How are ye, Tony? Don't ye know me?"

"Jack Wumble!" cried the old man. "How in the name o' fate did you git here?" And he lowered his gun and opened wide the door of the cabin for the old miner to enter.

CHAPTER XXVIII

AT TONY BINGS'S CABIN

Tony Bings was an old miner who had spent several years in Colorado, working close to Jack Wumble. The two knew each other well, and were warm friends.

"Come right in," said Tony Bings, when matters had been explained to him. "It's a wonder ye ain't friz stiff, in sech a wind! It's been a-blowin' great guns. Once or twice I thought the cabin was goin' over."

Tom was brought in and Sam followed, and both were placed near the sheet iron stove of which Tony Bings's cabin boasted. Then the old miner bustled about to get the whole party something to eat and to drink.

"I've got slathers o' stores," he told Jack Wumble, in answer to a question on that point. "Got a good supply in durin' the summer. I was out here last winter an' come near starvin' to de'th, an' I made up my mind it shouldn't happen ag'in. So eat yer fill an' welcome."

"We'll pay for all we use, Tony," answered

Wumble. "These chaps with me are rich," he added, in a whisper."

"At first I thought it might be some good-fer nuthin' fellers from up the mountains," went on Tony Bings. "Once in a while they come here and git things an' don't pay for 'em. If they come ag'in, I'll shoot 'em," he went on, with determination.

He listened with interest to the story the others had to relate, and was not surprised when he learned how the old hut had been tossed over by the tornado and carried along on the ice. He said his own shelter was protected by the rocks around it and also by the heavy stones which he had placed on the roof.

All of the newcomers were so exhausted that after eating their fill they were glad enough to lie down and rest. Tony Bings told them not to worry—that he would stay awake, to tend the fire and watch out generally.

"You ain't nowhere near Subler's Stores," he told Dick. "You got off the track entirely. Instead of going towards Dawson you've been goin' away from it."

All of the boys and Jack Wumble slept soundly that night. Tony Bings did not arouse them and consequently it was long past daylight when they opened their eyes.

When Dick came to the window of the cabin to look out he uttered a cry of surprise. The sun was shining and all around could be seen immense stretches of ice and snow. It looked as if they were in the midst of desolation.

"What a change from a week ago!" he said to Sam.

"A fellow could hardly believe it, Dick," was the reply.

"How do you feel?" went on the big brother.

"All right, only somewhat stiff."

Tom was still asleep. When he awoke the brothers were worried to see that he did not seem to be as clear in his mind as he had been the day before.

"Where is Ike Furner?" he asked, suddenly. "Say, I've got to be on my way, if I am going to get those nuggets of gold."

"Tom, take it easy," begged Dick. "Don't you remember me?" And he looked his brother full in the eyes.

"Sure I know you, Dick," was the wondering answer. "Why do you ask me such a question? Let me see, what was I saying?" Tom put his hand to his forehead. "Hang it all, it's slipped my mind entirely," he groaned.

"Never mind, Tom, let it go. You just think of Sam and me, and the folks at home. And don't forget Nellie," Dick added, in a whisper.

"Nellie!" gasped the sufferer. "Oh, yes, Nellie! As if I could ever forget her! Say, Dick, how soon will I see her, do you suppose?"

"I'll send for her as soon as we get home, Tom."

"And when will that be?"

"Oh, not so very long. Now do keep quiet. And don't think of anything but just home and Nellie," he added, pleadingly.

"All right, I'll do just as you want me to," returned Tom, and then laid back and was silent.

Sam had listened to what was going on and now he and Dick walked to the far end of the cabin, to talk in whispers.

"He isn't over it yet, Sam. And it almost looks as if he never would get over it, that is, altogether." Dick's face showed his deep concern.

"Oh, Dick, don't say that! He's got to get over it! Oh, if only we could get some first class doctor to do something!"

"Well, we've got to get to some city first—Dawson or some other place."

"Here is news!" cried Jack Wumble, coming forward at that instant. "Tony tells me that there will be a party going through to Dawson inside of a week or ten days. He advises that we wait till they go and go with 'em."

"It will be much safer," said Tony Bings. "It's a fearful journey alone—in sech weather."

"Who are those folks who are going?" asked Dick.

"One of the men who run the Yukon Supply Depot at Crovet, twenty-four miles from here. He will come along with four or five of his helpers, and most likely a dog train, and he always stops here."

"That will be all right—but a week or ten days—that's a long time to wait," and Dick sighed.

After that Tony Bings told his story, how he had come to that neighborhood and "struck it rich," as he confided to Jack Wumble. He was very enthusiastic about the diggings back of his cabin, and in the end got Wumble to promise to join him in his hunt for gold in the Spring.

"I've heard o' sech cases," he told the boys, after learning about Tom's trouble. "It's too bad! I sure do hope your brother will git over it. It ain't nice to have a crazy pusson in the family."

After that several days went by slowly. At times Tom seemed to improve and then he would sink back, sometimes becoming quite wild, so the others had to watch him closely. But he grew stronger physically, which was something to be thankful for.

On the third day it started to snow again, and this kept up for twenty-four hours. It was as cold as ever, and the sheet iron stove was kept almost red hot, so that the party, and especially Tom, might not take cold.

On the next morning, much to the surprise of everybody, Tom got up and insisted on walking around the cabin.

"I feel almost well," he told his brothers. "But I'd give a good deal to be home."

That afternoon came a great shouting, and the cracking of whips outside the cabin. At once Tony Bings's face lit up.

"It's the men from the Supply Depot!" he cried. "I reckon it's Schmidt."

"Hello, in dare!" was the cry. "Vos you alife alretty, Tony? Vy can't you oben der door und let a feller in, ain't it?"

"Hello, Gus!" answered the owner of the cabin, and threw open the door, and in bustled a big, fat German, heavily clad, and wearing thick gloves and ear-warmers. The newcomer stared in astonishment at the Rovers and Jack Wumble.

"Sure und I tidn't know you vos have combany, Tony," said Gus Schmidt.

"My friends," said the old miner, and introduced them. "Tell yer men to come in, and welcome," he went on, and Schmidt went to the door, and called to three men who were with him. They drove up with several dog teams, which they were taking to Dawson for supplies that had come up to that city by way of the Yukon River.

Gus Schmidt, despite his rather uncouth manner, was a whole-souled man, and Dick and the others took to him at once. He listened gravely to the story they had to tell, and readily agreed to take the Rovers and Jack Wumble with him. Wumble was invited by Tony Bings to remain at the cabin for the winter, but said he would first see the Rovers as far as Dawson, and visit his own claim, and then would return with Schmidt's party.

Of the newcomers one was a German like Schmidt and the other two were Canadians. The latter knew all about the dogs and dog sleds, managing the rather savage animals with scarcely an effort. The dogs had originally belonged to some Alaskan Indians and had cost the owners of the Supply Depot considerable money.

The start for Dawson, so many miles away, was made on the following morning. The boys and Jack Wumble shook hands with Tony Bings, who refused point blank to accept any money for what he had done for them. Tom was placed on one of the best of the big sleds and made as comfortable as circumstances permitted.

"All apoardt!" cried Gus Schmidt, gaily, and cracked the long whip he carried. The Canadians understood and cracked their own whips, and away went the whole party, over the fields of ice and snow, in the direction of Dawson.

CHAPTER XXIX

TOM'S WILD RIDE

"TALK about fields of ice, Dick! Just look around us!"

It was Sam who spoke. The party had come to a halt for the midday meal. They had stopped in the shelter of some big rocks, now thickly covered with snow and ice.

Snow and ice were on all sides—the latter glistening brightly in the sunshine. It was a wonderful transformation from the green and brown that had decked the landscape before winter had set in so suddenly.

"I'd hate to be out in this alone," remarked the big brother. "A fellow could get lost without half trying."

"Dick, what do you think of Tom?" went on Sam, in a lower tone.

"He's in a bad way again, Sam," was the reply. "Poor fellow! If only we had him where we could place him under the care of some good doctor, some specialist. That is what he needs."

Tom was indeed in a bad way. All morning he had talked in a rambling fashion, to himself and to the others around him. The Canadians were getting afraid of him and the Germans shrugged their shoulders.

"I dink he besser peen in an asylum, ain't it," said Gus Schmidt. "A feller can't vos dell vot such a feller vos going to do next alretty!"

"We'll have to watch him," had been Dick's answer.

One of the Canadians was preparing dinner, aided by one of the Germans. To show that they did not wish to shirk any camp duties, Sam and Dick did what they could to assist. The dogs and the sleds were off to one side. Tom sat on one sled, wrapped in heavy blankets, for it was still very cold.

Suddenly there came a wild shout from the Canadian who was doing the cooking. With a saucepan he pointed to the dogs and sleds. All of the others gazed in that direction and Sam and Dick set up a cry of alarm.

And well they might, for the sight that met their eyes filled them with fear. In some way Tom had gotten one of the sleds with its dogs away from the others and jumped aboard. With a crack of a whip he was off, standing on the sled and yelling like a demon.

"Tom! Tom! Stop!" screamed Dick and Sam in unison. "Come back here!"

"I'm off for gold! Nuggets of gold!" yelled the one who was not right in his mind. "Don't you dare to follow me! Off for gold! Gold! Gold!" And then the sled with its rider passed out of hearing, the dogs doing their best, urged on by the continued cracking of the long whip.

"We must catch him!" said Dick. "Quick! before he gets out of sight over some hill, or around some rocks!"

"He has der pest sled und der pest dogs!" groaned Gus Schmidt. "I said ve must keep an eye on him, yah! Of he busts dot sled somepody got to pay for him!"

"We'll pay, never fear," answered Sam. "But we must catch him! We don't want him to get hurt."

"You come mit me," said the leader of the outfit, motioning to Dick. "It ain't no use for all of us to go after him. De udders da stay right here. Ludvig, you hear?"

"Yah," came from the other German, and he nodded his head.

In a few minutes Gus Schmidt had one of the other dog teams ready for use. He was about to jump on the sled when he paused.

"Besser ve took somedings along," he suggested. "Somedings to eat und to trink, hey? Und some plankets, yah?" and he commenced to haul over the packs.

"Why, do you think the chase will be a long one?" asked Dick, anxiously.

"I can't vos tell dot. Mebbe him peen long. Dem vos schmart togs, I tole you dot."

A pack containing food and blankets was hastily thrown together and strapped to the sled. Then Dick was assigned a place and Gus Schmidt hopped aboard.

"Of ve ton't got back tonight go on to Riss Rifer," he directed the others.

"Good-by, Dick, and good luck!" called out Sam, and Jack Wumble waved his hand.

"You take care of yourself, Sam," was the brother's parting caution.

The dog sleds had done some fairly fast traveling before, but the rate of speed now set by Gus Schmidt almost took away Dick's breath. On and on bounded the sled, the dogs yelping wildly at first, but then settling down to a steady pace. Up one hill and down another they dashed, sending the loose snow flying in all directions. Soon the camp was left out of sight, even the smoke gradually disappearing from view.

Tom and his outfit were nowhere to be seen,

having long since passed over a hill to the northward. Gus Schmidt had, however, noted the direction with care. He had noted, too, that the runaway had taken a somewhat curved course, and now he attempted to catch him by taking a straight route for the same point.

For over an hour the chase kept up, and then, reaching the top of a long hill, they saw, far to the northward, a dog sled moving to the eastward.

"I dink I got him now!" cried Gus Schmidt, and once more he cracked his long whip and again his team bounded forward. Quarter of an hour passed and they drew closer to the other team, and then both the German and Dick set up a cry of dismay.

It was not the sled on which Tom had run away. The dogs were different and on the sled sat two men, strangers.

"Yes, we saw the sled you are after," said one of the men, when the others had come up and put a question to him and his companion. "It passed us, going like the wind and the driver yelling like a madman."

"And how was it headed?"

"About due North," answered the other man on the sled. And then he and his companion moved forward again.

"I dink ve haf to go pack und look for der tracks," said Gus Schmidt. "Too pad, dot vosn't our sled, ain't it?"

The team was turned back, and for the best part of half an hour they looked for the missing trail. At last it was discovered, and once more they moved rapidly forward, this time due North.

Fortunately there was little wind, otherwise Dick could not have stood that long and wild ride. As it was, he felt chilled to the bone, and his feet were like two lumps of ice. Gus Schmidt must have surmised this, for presently he stopped the sled and motioned to the youth.

"Ve git off und rundt a leetle. It vos do us goot," he remarked, and swung himself down on the icy snow. Dick followed, so stiff at first that he could scarcely put one foot before the other. They set off on a walk, the dogs pulling them, and gradually increased their speed to a run. Then Dick felt better.

All through the afternoon the chase kept up. They saw nothing of Tom. But the track he had left was a plain one and to that they stuck closely.

At last it grew so dark that they could see the track but indistinctly. They had to reduce their speed to a walk for fear of turning off.

"He ought to be stopping for the night," said Dick.

"Such a feller might not sthop at all," answered the German. "He might go on und on bis der togs trop dead, yah!"

Finally Gus Schmidt came to a halt and announced that they must go into camp for the night. The dogs needed the rest. They could continue the chase at the first sign of dawn.

"Do you know where we are?" asked Dick.

"Out in der ice und snow, dot ist all I know," said the German. "I nefer vos here pefore."

"If we are not lost we are next door to it," murmured Dick.

They had brought along a little tent and sleeping bags, and after supper made themselves as comfortable as possible. The dogs had been fed and they snapped and snarled over the bones thrown to them.

Only once during the night were Dick and his companion disturbed. From a distance came a yelping which the dogs at once answered.

"What is that?" asked the youth, sitting up. "Not the dogs of the other sled?"

"Nein, dot vos foxes," answered Gus Schmidt. "Ton't podder mit dem. Da ton't come here—da vos afraid of ter dogs." And he turned over to go to sleep again.

Dick could not sleep with any kind of comfort. He was utterly exhausted, yet his mind was continually on Tom. What was his poor brother doing, all by himself, amid that desolation of ice and snow?

At daybreak they were on the way again. The sun had come up, but soon it was hidden by a heavy bank of clouds, and then the snowflakes commenced to fall.

"Dot ist pad," said Gus Schmidt, shaking his head.

"You mean, it will wipe out the trail?" said Dick.

"Yah—der drail to find your prudder und der drail for us to git pack py. Maype ve besser go pack now."

"No! no! don't turn back! Please don't go back!" pleaded Dick. "He can't be so very far ahead of us. We are sure to catch up to him in a very short while now. If we——"

Dick did not finish, for a strange sight ahead caught his eye. Coming towards them was a dog team on a gallop. Behind the team was an overturned sled, empty.

CHAPTER XXX

GOOD-BYE TO ALASKA—CONCLUSION

"Is that your sled?"

"Yah. Vait, I vos sthop dem!" yelled Gus Schmidt, and with a dexterity that was really marvelous he turned his own team about and in a few seconds was traveling after the runaways.

"Wait! I'm going to get off! To look for my brother!" cried Dick, and as the German slackened his speed for a few seconds, the oldest Rover boy sprang out in the snow. He went sprawling, but was not injured. Almost before he knew it, the two sleds had disappeared and he was left alone.

All around him were the vast and mysterious fields of ice and snow. Far off he could hear the barking of the dogs, but this soon died out, and then came utter silence—a silence that seemed to fairly weigh him down. And now the snow started to come down harder than ever.

Had Dick Rover been less stout-hearted than he was he would have then and there given up the hunt for his brother. But Dick had the stuff of a real hero in him, and he went forward through the snow, bending low to escape the wind and to keep his eyes on that slowly disappearing trail.

Thus half an hour went by, and by that time, weighed down as he was by his heavy clothing and heavy footwear, Dick was well-nigh exhausted. He stopped to rest and to get his breath, and then, struck with a sudden idea, let out that old familiar locomotive whistle of Putnam Hall fame.

He waited for a few seconds and then whistled once more. Was he mistaken, or did an answering whistle sound out? He could not tell. He set his face grimly and trudged on.

At last he could see the trail no longer and then he realized the truth of the terrible situation.

He was lost on this vast field of ice and snow!

And Tom, somewhere ahead, must be lost, too!

It was a thought to make the stoutest heart quake. But Dick did not think of himself. He was thinking only of his brother. How could he locate Tom and save him from the cold and from starvation?

"I've got to do it!" he told himself, over and

over again. "I've got to do it! I must! I must!"

On and on he plunged, and suddenly went sprawling over some object half hidden in the falling snow. He felt around, and realized that he had come upon the two packs that had been on the sled Tom had taken.

"If they fell off here maybe Tom fell off, too!" he told himself. And then he commenced to search the vicinity carefully.

It was well that he did this, otherwise he might have missed poor Tom, who lay in a slight hollow, partly covered with snow. The sled had hit a rock and the poor youth had been flung out with great force, landing on one shoulder and on his head.

"Tom! Tom! Are you alive? Answer me!" cried Dick, as he raised his brother in his arms. But no reply came from Tom's lips. He was unconscious.

With all the strength that remained to him, Dick carried his brother to the spot where he had found the traps. Then he quickly undid the bundles, to see if there was anything there he might use. He found a tiny oil stove, filled with oil, and lit it, and then rolled Tom in two blankets, and gave him something hot to drink. Then he found a stick of wood, soaked it well in oil, and set it up in the ice as a torch.

All this while Tom lay like a log. He was breathing heavily, but he did not open his eyes or speak. Evidently the shock had been a heavy one. Dick did not know but what some of his brother's bones might be broken.

An anxious hour went by, and in that time Dick did all he could for Tom, who still laid in a stupor. Then came a shout, and Gus Schmidt appeared, driving his dog team and with the runaway team also in harness. Behind the first sled was the second—the one Tom had taken.

"So you got your brudder, hey?" said the German. "How vos he?"

"In bad shape, I'm afraid," answered Dick, soberly. "I guess the dogs ran away and pitched him overboard."

"I dink you vos right, und da drow dem dings oferpoard, doo," and Schmidt, pointed to the traps. "Vell, it's goot ve got der draps und er sled pack."

"Can we get back to the others tonight?"

"Nein, it was too dark und cold. Ve go in der morning, to Riss Rifer. Maybe dare you got a doctor, yah."

So it was settled, and the German proceeded to make himself and the others as comfortable as possible. He prepared something to eat, and suggested that Tom be given a little broth, made out of some dried meat. This was done, and presently the sufferer opened his eyes and tried to sit up.

"Whe—where in th—the world am I?" he asked, in a faint voice.

"Tom, you're all right," answered his brother, soothingly. "Do you know me?"

"Why, of course I know you," came the wondering answer. "What happened to me, Dick?"

"You ran off with a dog sled and got a nasty tumble."

"A dog sled? Dick, you are stringing me? Who's got a dog sled around Brill?"

"Never mind, Tom, just keep quiet. You're very sick. Just rest yourself."

"All right." Tom heaved a deep sigh. "Gosh! I do feel pretty bad!" he added. He had tried to sit up, but now fell back exhausted.

It was a night never to be forgotten. The German snored peacefully, but Dick did not close his eyes. He watched Tom closely, to do all he could for his brother and make certain that the sufferer should not get away again.

During the night it stopped snowing and in the morning the sun came out as brightly as ever. Dick was astir early, and was gratified to see that Tom was sleeping peacefully. They did not awaken the sufferer until Gus Schmidt announced himself ready to move on.

Tom was still very weak, but Dick was gratified to see that he appeared to be in his right mind, and his eyes were brighter than they had been in many a day.

"I can't understand this," he said, when he was bundled up and placed on one of the sleds. "I feel as if I had had some awful dream."

"So you have had, Tom," was Dick's reply. "And I want you to be careful, so that that awful dream doesn't come back."

"But where are we, Dick?"

"In Alaska, Tom. Now do keep quiet, please."

"Alaska! Well, I never!" murmured the sufferer. "And I thought we were near Brill, or the farm!"

The two boys occupied the rear sled with one of the bundles, while Gus Schmidt did the driving from the other sled and carried the rest of the traps. On and on they went, mile after mile, the German driving the dogs with great skill. They passed over hill after hill, and over vast expanses of ice and snow. At noon they rested half an hour for lunch. Tom tried to stand up, but was too weak.

"It's no use, Dick," he said. "I'm about as

strong as a bowl of mush! I guess I need about a month's rest."

"And you are going to get it, Tom, as soon as we can get home," replied his brother.

"But I don't understand how I got here," went on the sufferer, in perplexity.

"I'll tell you all about it some day, Tom. But now you must keep quiet. Won't you, just to please me?"

"Sure—anything you say, Dick. I know something is wrong somewhere. But I'll leave it all to you."

Late that evening they reached the Riss River, a small stream flowing into the mighty Yukon. They passed along the river bank until they reached a settlement known as Boyer's. Here they found Sam and the others of the expedition.

"So yer got Tom!" cried Jack Wumble. "Good enough!"

"And how is he?" questioned Sam, anxiously.

"He's been hurt, Sam. But I think he is brighter in his mind than ever," answered Dick.

The Rovers found a great bustle and confusion going on at Boyer's depot, due to the fact that a steamer coming down the river from Dawson was due the next morning. It was to be the last vessel to pass that way until Spring.

"Where is that steamer bound for?" asked Dick, of the man who had charge of the depot.

"San Francisco."

"Can we secure passage on her, do you think?"

"I reckon so. Travel is light this time of year. That boat is going to have some trouble getting through the ice, though."

"We'll risk that—if only they will take us on board."

The party was made as comfortable as possible at Boyer's, sharing various bunks in a cabin that chanced to be deserted. Dick settled up with Gus Schmidt, stating he would not go on to Dawson if he could secure passage on the steamer.

At last the vessel came in, and after the general hubub was over Dick inquired about accommodations.

"Pretty full, but I think we can stow you away somewhere," said the purser.

"I don't care what sort of accommodations we have, so long as my brother gets a stateroom," went on Dick. "He isn't very well."

"Bring your baggage aboard, and I'll fix you up somehow, later on."

The boys went aboard the steamer and there

bid farewell to Jack Wumble. They had left some things at Dawson, and these they turned over, on a written order, to the old miner, telling him to do as he pleased with them.

"Good-bye to ye!" cried Wumble, on parting. "An' good luck," he added, and shook hands all around.

After the rough experiences in the wilds of Alaska, the boys felt quite at home on the big steamer. The purser managed to find a large stateroom for them, containing three berths. And, what was even better, he introduced Dick and Sam to a doctor who chanced to be on board. The physician was a man of experience, who lived in San Francisco, and he readily agreed to take Tom under his care and do all he could for the sufferer.

"I think all he needs is rest—absolute rest," said the doctor, after an examination. "He ought not to go to college again—at least, not for a year or two."

"It's hard to keep him quiet, Doctor—he has always been such a lively fellow—the liveliest boy in our family," said Dick.

"Well, then, let him travel. Anything to keep his mind from his books and from himself."

The voyage down the mighty Yukon to Bering Sea and the Pacific Ocean was a long and tedious one to Dick and Sam. For several days the steamer had a hard time of it, crushing her way through the ice, which was rapidly forming. In a few days more navigation would be completely closed, so far as that portion of our globe was concerned.

"We got out just in time," said Dick to Sam, when the Yukon was at last left behind and they saw ahead of them the blue waters of Bering Sea.

The trip on the ocean seemed to do Tom a world of good. Daily he grew stronger, until he could walk on deck. The doctor attended him from time to time, but gave the sufferer little medicine.

As soon as it was possible to do so, Dick sent a wireless message ashore, to be relayed to the farm, telling the folks that Tom was safe and that all hands would soon be back at Valley Brook. This message was also sent, by way of the farm, to Mrs. Stanhope and Dora, and to the girls at Hope.

"My gracious, what adventures we have had on this trip!" remarked Sam to Dick, as the steamer was headed for the Golden Gate, the entrance to San Francisco harbor.

"Right you are, Sam," was the reply. "I

don't think we'll have any more so strenuous." But Dick was mistaken. More adventures were still in store for the Rovers, and what some of them were will be related in the next volume of this series, to be entitled "The Rover Boys in Business; Or, The Search for the Missing Bonds."

On the arrival at San Francisco it was deemed advisable by the doctor that Tom rest for a few days at a hotel before starting on the trip for home. Tom's mind now seemed to be as clear as ever and all his weakness was physical.

One day, when Dick was reading a local newspaper, he chanced on a paragraph that instantly arrested his attention. He read it carefully and then sought out Sam.

"Look here," he cried. "Here is news about that lady on the train who lost her handbag with jewelry in it worth ten thousand dollars."

"What about it?" asked Sam, with interest.

"She didn't lose it at all, it seems. Her mother, who was with her, took it and absent-mindedly hid it in their berth. There a porter found it and turned it over to the railroad company."

"Well, that clears Tom of that," said Sam, with a sigh of relief. "But what of Hiram Duff's money and jewelry?"

"That still remains to be found out, Sam. I guess Tom took it—but of course he didn't know what he was doing. You can't count such a thing a crime when a fellow is out of his mind."

In the end, it may be as well to state here, this mystery was never fully explained. But the Rover family paid the old miser for his loss, and for what he had suffered in being locked down in his cellar; and there the matter was dropped.

Tom stood the journey to Valley Brook better than expected. At the Oak Run railroad station the family touring car was drawn up, with Jack Ness, the hired man, in charge. The boys' father was there to greet them.

"My boys! My boys!" he said, and the tears stood in his eyes. Then he folded poor Tom in his arms and led him to the touring car. And there a surprise awaited the sufferer. Nellie was there, having arrived the day before from Hope.

"I just had to come," she said, and then she caught Tom and held him tightly. The tears were streaming down her cheeks, and the others had to turn away. "Oh, Tom! Tom!" she murmured, over and over again.

"Oh, Nellie, don't make such a fuss! I'm not worth it!" murmured Tom, but, nevertheless, he looked greatly pleased. "I've had a—an awful —dream," he went on, slowly. "But I'm—well,

I'm not going to dream that way again—not if I can help it!" And he gave her a look that thrilled her through and through.

There was another warm welcome when the touring car reached the farm. Uncle Randolph and Aunt Martha were on the piazza to meet the boys. Aunt Martha shed tears over Tom, just as Nellie had done, but they were tears of joy and nobody minded them. Uncle Randolph shook hands, and told them all to come in out of the cold, and rubbed his own hands together in great satisfaction.

"Home again!" murmured Tom, when he stood in the great hallway. He gave a deep sniff. "And a good dinner! Aunt Martha, you know how to make us feel comfortable, don't you?" He gave her one of his old-time hugs. His eyes were as clear as they had ever been. Evidently he was fast becoming the Tom of old. His running away from Brill, and his trip to Alaska, were but a horrible, uncertain nightmare to him. He did not want to remember those days, and they were best forgotten.

"And how do you feel, Dad?" asked Dick, as soon as he could get the chance.

"Better than in many a day," returned Anderson Rover.

"And what is the news from New York?"

"Everything is going along well. We have those brokers just where we want them."

"Good! That is what I like to hear," and Dick's face showed his satisfaction.

"I've got more news, Dick, that you will like to hear," said his father, with a faint smile.

"What is that?"

"Dora telegraphed that she would be here to-night."

"Fine!"

"Well, we certainly had a great trip," said Sam, when the whole family and Nellie were gathered around the dining table. "But I don't know as I want to take it over again."

"Hardly," returned his big brother.

THE END